NoLcx 1/13

PRINCE OF
HUMBUGS

Quest for a King
Searching for the Real King Arthur

Kindred Spirit
A Biography of L. M. Montgomery

Prince of Humbugs
A Life of P. T. Barnum

PRINCE OF HUMBUGS

A LIFE OF
P.T. BARNUM

CATHERINE M. ANDRONIK

ATHENEUM 1994 NEW YORK
Maxwell Macmillan Canada
Toronto
Maxwell Macmillan International
New York Oxford Singapore Sydney

FOR F. M.

Atheneum
Macmillan Publishing Company
866 Third Avenue
New York, NY 10022

Maxwell Macmillan Canada, Inc.
1200 Eglinton Avenue East
Suite 200
Don Mills, Ontario M3C 3N1

Macmillan Publishing Company is part of the
Maxwell Communication Group of Companies.

First edition
Printed in the United States of America
10 9 8 7 6 5 4 3 2 1
The text of this book is set in 11 point Bembo

Andronik, Catherine M.
Prince of Humbugs : the life of P. T. Barnum / by Catherine M.
Andronik ; illustrated with prints and photographs.
p.   cm.
Includes bibliographical references and index.
ISBN 0-689-31796-4
1. Barnum, P. T. (Phineas Taylor), 1810–1891—Juvenile literature.
2. Circus owners—United States—Biography—Juvenile literature.
[1. Barnum, P. T. (Phineas Taylor), 1810–1891. 2. Circus owners.]
I. Title.
GV1811.B3A53   1994
338.7'617913'092—dc20
[B]   93-36724
SUMMARY:
A biography of the life of Phineas Taylor Barnum

ACKNOWLEDGMENTS

When I moved to Fairfield, Connecticut, I was vaguely aware that I was in Barnum territory, but didn't pay much attention to the fact until I was asking an acquaintance for directions to the Klein Auditorium in Bridgeport. "Turn left on 'Aaronstan,' " she said. So I drove along looking for the street—and the closest I could find was Iranistan *Avenue. How, I wondered, did a street with a name like that turn up in the middle of Bridgeport? My search for an answer led me to P. T. Barnum.*

It also led me to some wonderfully helpful people who spend their days keeping the showman's memory alive. My thanks go out to Mary Witkowski for her guidance through the maze of the Historical Collection at the Bridgeport Public Library, and to Robert Pelton at the Barnum Museum for his guided tour of that fascinating little jewel in the heart of the city.

P. T. Barnum loved to write about himself as much as he loved to be written about by other people. Most of the quotations I've used in this book are taken from a compilation and condensation of his many autobiographies, Barnum's Own Story: The Autobiography of P. T. Barnum.

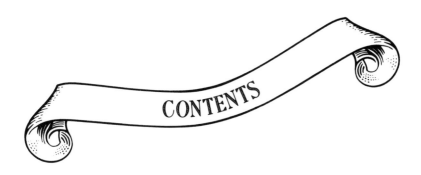

CONTENTS

P. T. Barnum was a man with big ideas—and the drive to make them reality. (Historical Collection, Bridgeport Public Library)

DEAL OF A LIFETIME

YOU MAY HAVE HEARD CONNECTICUT CALLED THE NUTMEG State, and people from Connecticut called Nutmeggers. The nickname started out as a sort of insult from colonial times, when peddlers would travel around New England with their wagons, selling everything from nails to whole nutmegs—hard little seeds that were ground up to make a sharp spice. People said to watch out for peddlers from Connecticut, because they had a reputation for being cunning and not always trustworthy salesmen. They could talk people into buying almost anything, convincing them that they'd gotten a wonderful bargain. They could even sell unsuspecting housewives big, beautiful, perfect nutmegs—carved from wood.

There was one young man living in New York City in 1835 who would not have considered being called a Nutmegger an insult. In fact, he would have taken it as a completely appropriate compliment! His name was Phineas Taylor Barnum, and he had come to the city from Bethel, Connecticut. Young Barnum had worked in his family's store, so he was well acquainted with the unscrupulous realities of buying and selling. Perhaps people in his day no longer tried to deal in wooden nutmegs, but it was easy to make a sack of potatoes a pound or two heavier—and more expensive— by adding a few rocks. The whole Barnum family also loved to play practical jokes, which was unusual in strict, serious nineteenth-century New England. While he shifted from job to job, barely able to support himself and his family, Barnum knew that, somehow, his true calling would combine the talents he'd inherited, the things he'd practiced and loved all his life: selling and entertaining. But he couldn't imagine what that ideal career could be.

Then, while he was writing publicity notices for a New York theater, he heard some news that would change his life— and the world—forever: Scudder's American Museum was for sale. The museum was a motley collection of stuffed bird and animal specimens, historical artifacts, and pieces of art, all unimaginatively exhibited in a dull marble building on the corner of Broadway and Ann Street in New York City. Mr. Scudder had died, leaving the museum to his daughters. They had no idea how to manage it or attract visitors; it was losing rather than making money, and they had no choice but to sell the collection quickly.

Barnum had strolled through the museum a few times, just out of curiosity. He liked to look at unusual and exotic things. Now, however, he returned to look at the displays again from a very different perspective. And what he saw was his chance for fame and fortune. The museum, he thought, held rich possibilities, given a few strategic changes and some aggressive advertising. Barnum knew he was the man to turn the old museum into one of the wonders of New

York—maybe even of the world; and he was determined to buy it.

There was one obstacle, though—a large one. The price of the museum was fifteen thousand dollars. And P. T. Barnum was practically penniless.

Still, Barnum began to tell his friends that Scudder's Museum would soon be his. What, they wanted to know, was he planning on using for money? "Brass," young Barnum replied, meaning sheer audacity—"for silver and gold I have none."

Barnum, of course, had a plan—seldom in his life would he be without one! The Scudder daughters owned the museum collection, but they only rented the building that housed it. The landlord, Barnum discovered, was a Mr. Olmsted. Barnum paid Olmsted a visit, armed with an attractive business proposal. If Olmsted would buy the collection of Scudder's American Museum for twelve thousand dollars, Barnum would manage it. Each month, he would make a payment to Olmsted, until the whole sum was repaid. Then the museum would be his. A single late payment, and Barnum would lose all claim to the enterprise.

Olmsted liked the idea, and he was intrigued by the brash young man who'd dreamed it up. But running a museum was a complicated business, and Barnum had no reputation in New York's business community. So Olmsted asked Barnum to send by a few of the men he'd worked for as references, proof of his ability and character. Most of Barnum's odd jobs had been in theaters and in taverns featuring entertainment; these were the employers he contacted, asking them to visit Mr. Olmsted and put in a good word for him.

A few days later, Olmsted called Barnum back to his office. To Barnum's dismay, Olmsted began by saying that he hadn't liked all those references from the entertainment world. Then he explained: They had all spoken so highly of young Barnum's ability to bring in money, Olmsted suspected they were in on the deal!

There was just one final detail to clear up. The investment *was* a big one, and Barnum wasn't contributing a penny. Olmsted wanted *something* as security from Barnum, something to guarantee that he would recoup some of his money in case things didn't go as planned. Was there, he wondered, a bank account, a home, a piece of land to serve as collateral?

And Barnum thought: Ivy Island.

Back in Bethel, Connecticut, Barnum's grandfather, Phineas Taylor, had been a major landowner. The boy inherited both his name and his sense of humor—and something more, too. When Barnum was a small child, Grandfather Taylor signed over a piece of land called Ivy Island to his grandson. He grew up hearing that he was a landowner like his grandfather, and he could hardly wait to see *his* property. He imagined a green island, rich and beautiful, set in the middle of a sparkling blue lake. Finally, when he was eleven, his grandfather took him to see his land. It was a once-in-a-lifetime trip—literally—for young Barnum never wanted to go back. Ivy Island turned out to be a snake-infested thicket surrounded by swamp, utterly useless for building or farming. To the family, it was a hilarious hoax, a trick on a boy who luckily had a good sense of humor.

But Mr. Olmsted didn't know that. And so, the "worthless" land Barnum had ignored for years, the biggest practical joke of his childhood, was about to help finance his dream.

Then, with Scudder's American Museum nearly in his grasp, disaster struck. The directors of the New York Museum Company, who already owned the rival Peale's Museum, had just bid on Scudder's, and their offer was higher than Barnum's. The dusty stuffed animals and cases of relics were theirs.

At that point, most men would have given up and moved on to another pursuit. P. T. Barnum, however, was not like most men. Well trained himself in the art of deception, he sensed something not quite right about that competing bid, and he started investigating. The directors of the Museum Company, he discovered, included men who had reputations of leading businesses—a bank in one case—into ruin, then walking away comfortably. They avoided responsibility for their ruined companies by selling stocks. When the projects failed, the *stockholders* would be the ones to lose money. And Scudder's Museum would fail, for the buyers had no interest in updating or maintaining it.

Armed with this damaging information, Barnum wrote letter after scathing letter to city newspapers, exposing the plan just as the stock went on the market. Needless to say, no one would dream of buying stock in the former Scudder's American Museum.

Barnum's competitors recognized that they were dealing with a potentially dangerous enemy. They hoped they could make him a friend and silence his bad publicity by offering him a job with them as manager of the museum. Barnum accepted the offer, and the letters ceased. But Barnum's plot was far from finished.

Barnum learned that the Museum Company owed a payment on Scudder's on December 26. He made secret arrangements that, if the payment were late by as much as a day, the sale would fall through and his earlier, lower bid would be accepted. He was counting on his ability to lull the competition into a false sense of security—and he succeeded. With Barnum apparently content and out of the way, the Museum Company didn't think it was important to make its payment promptly. December 26 came and went, and at 10:00 A.M. on December 27, Barnum and an attorney were at Mr. Olmsted's door, ready to change Scudder's to Barnum's American Museum at last.

One of the first things Barnum did as owner of the museum was to send a letter to the directors of the New York Museum Company, offering them lifetime free admission to his establishment.

Barnum was determined to repay his debt to Olmsted quickly. To do that, he had to make Barnum's American Museum a rousing success, an unparalleled crowd-pleaser. He remodeled, rearranged, decorated, advertised, updated with the latest technology, booked exciting attractions, advertised some more, stretched the truth to the most tempting point of incredibility, advertised still more—and happily watched as crowds arrived skeptical and left smiling. And as he spent money lavishly on the museum, he saved in his personal life. Barnum and his wife and baby daughter were somehow surviving in New York City on a budget of six hundred dollars a year, living in a single small room that had previously been a billiard parlor! One day, six months after buying the museum, Mr. Olmsted visited the offices at dinnertime. He found Barnum sitting at his desk, munching on a cold sandwich. He explained that he ate only one hot meal a week with his family, and that was Sunday dinner. He'd continue to be frugal, he vowed, until he'd fully repaid Olmsted for his investment.

In just a little over a year, the twelve-thousand-dollar debt was paid, and the American Museum officially belonged to P. T. Barnum.

One miracle deal like this would be the dream of a lifetime for most businessmen. P. T. Barnum made such deals a habit.

In his eighty-one years, Barnum would be known as a pro-moter of frauds and Prince of Humbugs, a patron of the fine arts, a showman of legendary proportions, a politician, a philanthropist, an author, an advertiser, an innovator, a self-proclaimed citizen of "the Universal Yankee Nation," even a preacher of sorts. But he saw himself as a classic Nutmegger: a man who could sell a wooden nutmeg *and* convince the buyer that a wooden nutmeg was a fine thing to own indeed.

Barnum made the American Museum one of the principal attractions of nineteenth-century New York. (Barnum Museum, Bridgeport)

"THE LAZIEST BOY IN TOWN"

BETHEL, CONNECTICUT, IS A SMALL, RURAL TOWN IN THE state's southwest corner, where gentle hills roll down to the Long Island Sound coastline. In 1810, the year its most famous native was born, Bethel had not yet become a town in its own right. It was still part of the city of Danbury, known worldwide for its hat factories.

Many of Bethel's farmers had owned their land for generations. Among them were the Barnums. Back in the 1600s, twelve-year-old Thomas Barnum wanted to leave England and settle in America. But the voyage was expensive and—like his famous descendant two centuries later—he had no money. Thomas Barnum financed his trip by becoming an indentured servant: He promised to work for a master for several years once he got to America. Gradually, he would pay off the price of his passage and buy his freedom. Also like his descendant, he was a determined worker. By 1685, Thomas Barnum was not only a free man, he was also one of the founders of Danbury. A later Barnum, Ephraim, was a captain in the American Revolution. His son Philo was a tailor, farmer, taverner, and storekeeper. When Philo Barnum married Irena Taylor, he was a widower with five children.

The Taylors were another old, prosperous Bethel family. Irena's father, Phineas, had been elected twice to the Connecticut state legislature. He owned many acres of farmland, and was considered a rich man by his neighbors. He also had a reputation as a practical joker. According to P. T. Barnum, Phineas Taylor "would go farther, wait longer, work harder and contrive deeper, to carry out a practical joke, than for anything else under heaven."

Phineas Taylor, P. T. Barnum's grandfather, was a notorious practical joker. (from Barnum's Own Story)

Once, Phineas Taylor was traveling by boat from Norwalk, Connecticut, to New York City with a number of businessmen. The voyage across Long Island Sound ordinarily took eight hours. But the weather was strange; the wind failed, and the boat was becalmed for five days. After nearly a week, the once clean-shaven businessmen had grown rather scruffy beards. Not one had thought of bringing along a razor—except, strange coincidence, for Phineas Taylor. When the boat finally got under way, Taylor announced that he had a fair plan to get everyone shaved with just one razor. Each man would shave half his face, then pass the razor on to the next man. When all were half shaved, the rotation would begin again. They were at Taylor's mercy, so the men agreed. All went smoothly at first, and after everyone was half shaved the razor returned to Taylor. He finished shaving, then told his companions that the blade was dull and needed sharpening. Old-fashioned razors were honed by striking them against a leather strap. As Taylor whipped the blade back and forth, it suddenly flew out of his hand—and fell into the depths of Long Island Sound. It was a curious sight when the boat docked in New York and its passengers sheepishly disembarked, every man neatly shaved on one side of his face, whiskered on the other—except for sly Phineas Taylor.

On the fifth of July, the day after Independence Day, 1810, a baby boy was born to Philo and Irena Taylor Barnum. They named him Phineas Taylor, after his jokester grandfather. This delighted the old man so much he was inspired to play another practical joke and present his grandson with that magnificent piece of real estate, Ivy Island. Grandfather Taylor was young Taylor's role model as he grew up; he taught him to make people laugh at themselves.

As he became famous, P. T. Barnum had no regrets that he'd just missed being a firecracker July 4 baby.

I'd have enjoyed being born on the Fourth of July, but maybe my tardiness was for the best. Competition between Barnum and Independence Day would have been too much. As it was, I made my appearance after peace and quiet had been restored and the audience had regained its seats.

Young Taylor Barnum "had the reputation of being the laziest boy in town," because he spent more time finding ways to avoid the usual farm chores than the chores themselves would take. He was not cut out to be a farmer. "I always disliked work. Head-work I was excessively fond of. I was always ready to concoct fun, or lay plans for money-making, but hand-work was decidedly not in my line." Before he was twelve, Taylor Barnum was already a business entrepreneur, making a few pennies by selling cherry-flavored rum to thirsty militiamen after their drills and parades.

You might expect someone who liked "head-work" to excel in school. Taylor was a good student, especially in mathematics, but he was not exceptional. He attended the local public school, then spent one term at Danbury Academy, which was like a high school. That was the end of the formal education of Phineas Taylor Barnum.

In 1825, Philo Barnum, Taylor's father, died. He left many debts, but no money with which to pay them. The children from his first marriage were grown, with families of their own to support. As Irena's oldest child, it was up to Taylor to keep his mother and four younger brothers and sisters from starving. He went to work in his uncle's store in Grassy Plain, a mile from the Bethel homestead. For the next several years, while he occasionally dabbled in other pursuits, P. T. Barnum made his living as a storekeeper in various places.

Barnum may have been the head of his family now, responsible for its welfare, but he was still trying to think up novel ways to make money while avoiding work. In one of the stores where he clerked, Barnum discovered that there were some customers who did their shopping very early in the morning, when he'd rather sleep. Each night, he'd tie a string around one of his toes, hang the other end out the window of his room above the store, and leave a sign telling early-morning customers to pull the string for service. He'd jump out of bed at the first pull, wait on the shopper, then go back to bed until another customer tweaked his toe.

Young Barnum also had some creative business ideas that sounded crazy to his employers—until the ideas worked. One day, a traveling salesman arrived at the store. He sold Barnum a huge, utterly useless load of small green glass bottles. They'd been incredibly cheap—but the store owner wasn't impressed. There was no way they'd sell so many little bottles. But Barnum, as always, had a plan.

Lotteries were popular fund-raisers in Connecticut at the time. People have always liked the idea of paying a few pennies for the chance to win large prizes. Not long after Barnum bought the bottles, customers in the shop where he worked were greeted by a flamboyant sign. The store, it announced, was holding a lottery. Just by buying a fifty-cent ticket, anybody could win a handsome prize consisting of selected store merchandise. Out of the one thousand tickets that would be sold, there would be over five hundred winners. It would be easier to win than lose! The lucky tickets were drawn, and winners began to arrive to claim their prizes. And, except for the cash grand prize, the winnings *did* consist of selected store merchandise, as promised: assorted green glass bottles, kitchen gadgets that hadn't moved from the storeroom in years, and an occasional really useful item. After Barnum's lottery, not only were all the bottles gone, so was most of the store's old, hard-to-sell inventory. And, like a true Nutmegger, Barnum made the winners feel that they were getting *exactly* what they'd paid for.

While Barnum was working in Grassy Plain, he faithfully traveled the mile home to Bethel every Saturday night to spend Sunday with his mother. One summer Saturday, a young Bethel seamstress named Charity Hallett had come to Grassy Plain to buy a new hat from the shop owned by Barnum's landlady's daughter. By evening, it had turned stormy, and Charity, frightened by the thunder and the dark, was looking for a traveling companion back to Bethel. When his landlady mentioned the problem, Taylor Barnum agreed to accompany Miss Hallett. It was truly love at first sight. Barnum was soon going out of his way to see the young woman whose beauty he'd first glimpsed in a flash of lightning.

Barnum and Charity began to discuss marriage. Their families, however, were opposed. The Halletts were not impressed by the young man who was so seriously courting their daughter: a teenage store clerk with thick, curly hair, a large, bulbous nose, and skin badly scarred from a recent bout of smallpox. Besides, Charity was two years older than Barnum. The Barnums, on the other hand, felt that their Taylor could find a younger girl, perhaps someone with a more prestigious job than a seamstress.

In November of 1829, Charity was visiting an uncle in New York City. Barnum used the excuse of a business trip to meet her there. On November 8, P. T. Barnum and Charity Hallett were very quietly married. While their families were angry for a while about the secrecy, eventually they came to accept the young couple. Barnum was nineteen years old; Charity was twenty-one.

With a wife to support, Barnum tried to settle down in Bethel and establish himself as a storekeeper who sold, according to his own advertisement, "all kinds of dry goods, groceries, crockery, etc., 25 per cent. cheaper than any of his neighbors." But there were so many more interesting and exciting things to do than run a general store!

In the mid-1800s, almost anyone with a strong opinion and the money to afford it published a newspaper, and P. T.

Barnum escorted Charity Hallett home in a thunderstorm—and fell in love. They were married in 1829. (Historical Collection, Bridgeport Public Library)

Barnum was no exception. Small towns in New England were notoriously conservative. They adhered strictly to the somber rules of the old Congregational church and the powerful local politicians the church supported. Barnum might have been a son and citizen of quiet little Bethel, but the most influential person in his life had been liberal, independent-thinking Grandfather Taylor. Barnum saw and disliked some of the unfair practices of the local church and government officials, and he criticized them in his own newspaper, the *Herald of Freedom*, starting in October of 1831. Before long, the things Barnum was printing were offending some important, powerful people.

Three times in the three years he published the paper, Barnum was brought to court on the charge of libel: printing malicious, harmful statements about another person, statements the accused said were lies. Each time, Barnum had chosen his words to say exactly what he meant, and he wasn't about to retract them. In 1832, his stubborn criticism landed him in jail.

In his paper, Barnum accused a prominent local minister of usury, or charging an unfairly high rate of interest on a loan. Usury is a crime specifically condemned in the Bible, so God-fearing New Englanders were especially sensitive to such a charge. Barnum was brought to court and found guilty of libel. His sentence was a one-hundred-dollar fine and sixty days in the Danbury jail, which he served in flamboyant style. Barnum had his jail cell attractively carpeted and wallpapered, and he made certain he would spend his two months there comfortably, with good meals and plenty of reading and writing to occupy himself.

On the day Barnum was released, he arranged for a huge celebration. A brass band played as he stepped outdoors and into a fine horse-drawn coach. He was escorted the three miles from Danbury to Bethel by the band, forty men on horseback, and sixty carriages full of local supporters. When he arrived at his home, the band played its final, sentimental tune: "Home, Sweet Home." Barnum was learning to turn *anything* into an event, an extravaganza, to attract attention.

The Barnums' first daughter, Caroline, was born in 1833. The following year, business was bad in the Bethel store, and Barnum decided to try his luck in New York City. The employment situation was bad there, too, and he found himself struggling to make ends meet, working on and off in a variety of jobs, anything from tending bar to writing publicity notices for theaters.

The show business connections Barnum made would soon serve him well, for his fortune was ready to change. P. T. Barnum was about to meet Joice Heth, the 160-year-old woman.

3

THE 160-YEAR-OLD WOMAN

PEOPLE HAVE ALWAYS BEEN FASCINATED BY THINGS THAT ARE
odd, or extraordinary, or weird. In Barnum's day, unusual
people like giants, or dwarfs, or bearded ladies were exhibited
by showmen for money. Some of the exhibits were dehu-
manizing sideshows where spectators came to stare and jeer.
But others were in a different class. The audience would meet
the unusual person in a comfortable setting where he or she
could speak or perform and answer questions. It was news
of one of these exhibits that sparked Barnum's professional
showman's instincts for the first time.

While he was struggling to make a living in New York
City, Barnum ran into an old Connecticut acquaintance,
Coley Bartram. Bartram and a Mr. Lindsay had been the
managers of a very unusual woman then on display in Philadelphia. Bartram had recently sold out his share, though,
and Lindsay, too, was getting tired of the project. Would
Barnum be interested, he wondered, in taking over the management of the extraordinary Joice Heth?

Joice Heth was a black woman who appeared to be, not just old, or even very old, but positively ancient. She was almost totally paralyzed; the only part of her body she could still move was one hand with its four-inch-long, horny nails. Her gnarled toenails were a quarter of an inch thick. Old Joice, who weighed only forty-six pounds, may have been toothless and blind, but her mind was sharp, and she loved to talk. And what she talked about was more astounding than her appearance.

According to her story, she'd been born in 1674, making her over 160 years old! Coley Bartram even had a document to prove her age: a bill of sale, dated 1727, for a slave named Joice Heth. Still more incredible were Joice Heth's former owners. The bill of sale said she had been a slave of Augustine Washington of Virginia—the father of George Washington! As a young woman, Joice had been nurse and nanny to the infant future president. She delighted in telling her audience stories about "little George"—details only someone closely connected to the Washingtons could have known.

Barnum hurried to Philadelphia, saw Joice Heth for himself, and paid Coley Bartram one thousand dollars for the rights to exhibit the 160-year-old woman. He had to borrow the money, but he was certain he'd earn it back easily with his new client.

Barnum wanted to exhibit Joice Heth in New York City, and he wanted a respectful and respectable show in a good establishment. One of the men Barnum had applied to work for as a bartender (although he didn't get the job) was William Niblo, who ran Niblo's Garden, a fashionable saloon/restaurant/entertainment hall. When Niblo heard a description of the withered old woman, he didn't think his more squeamish customers would enjoy seeing her while they ate and drank. But he agreed that people would be interested in her. He leased Barnum a small room just off the main "garden." There, Barnum set up Joice Heth's exhibit area, where she would lie comfortably on a large couch.

Barnum hired Levi Lyman, a lawyer who would help him with publicity for many years, to put together a booklet of Joice Heth's "memoirs." The two men advertised "Aunt Joice" with newspaper ads and eye-catching posters. Strict Congregationalists—in other words, most Americans in the early 1800s—were raised believing that it was sinful to seek out entertainment for its own sake. So Barnum emphasized Joice Heth's connections with the Washington family. That way, audiences could feel they were being educated by a living piece of history. Joice Heth also loved to sing old hymns, and knew more verses than anyone in the audience, which appealed to people's religious sensibilities. Barnum learned a lesson from Joice Heth that he would always remember: Give the public fun and amazement, but convince them that they're seeing something educational and morally uplifting, too.

Crowds flocked to Niblo's Garden to see Joice Heth, to marvel at her amazing age, and to hear her stories about the young George Washington. Months went by when Joice Heth pulled in as much as fifteen hundred dollars a week for P. T. Barnum. But, inevitably, the novelty eventually wore off and the crowds grew smaller and smaller. It was time, Barnum decided, to get the show on the road. Boston was Joice Heth's next stop.

Once again, the ancient woman was a favorite attraction for many weeks. Then, just as the crowds were beginning to diminish, a letter appeared in a local newspaper. Some shows and museums were exhibiting extremely lifelike mechanical mannequins made of metal and rubber. The robotlike machines could be manipulated to move like human beings,

THE GREATEST
Natural & National
CURIOSITY
IN THE WORLD.

JOICE

HETH,

Nurse to Gen GEORGE WASHINGTON, (the Father of our Country,) WILL BE SEEN AT

Barnum's Hotel, Bridgeport,

Barnum became a showman when he exhibited Joice Heth, the 160-year-old nurse of George Washington. (Courtesy of Somers Historical Society, Somers, New York)

and even seemed to talk—with the aid of a ventriloquist. Edgar Allan Poe would expose such a mechanical fraud: a chess-playing "automaton" with a cleverly concealed human operator. The letter in the Boston newspaper claimed that Joice Heth, too, was an automaton: lifelike, but manufactured. Immediately, hundreds of people who had already seen the old woman returned to puzzle over whether she was human or machine, wondering if they had been fooled. It was never proved, but it's suspected that Barnum himself wrote and sent that letter. He knew very well that people can't resist a good mystery.

After traveling around New England from city to city, Joice Heth became ill. Barnum sent her to his brother's home in Bethel, where she received the best of care. Despite the nursing, the old woman died on February 19, 1836. Barnum had already agreed that, when Joice Heth died, he would allow a doctor to perform an autopsy, since a woman who could live to the age of 162 would surely be of interest to science. The body was rushed to New York City, where Dr. David L. Rogers began his examination, before a paying audience of doctors, medical students, newspaper editors, and Barnum himself. The results were shocking. Externally, Joice Heth really did look 162 years old. But her arteries and internal organs were in remarkably good condition for a woman of that extraordinary age. Dr. Rogers estimated that, in fact, Joice Heth was not much older than eighty. The public had been fooled.

In some of his future endeavors, Barnum would exaggerate in his advertising or exhibit things he knew were fakes. But in the case of Joice Heth, he really *had* believed that she was 162 years old. Didn't he have the yellowed bill of sale to prove it? Of course, the bill may have referred to some other seventeenth-century slave named Joice Heth—but Barnum had been utterly convinced that old Aunt Joice was authentic.

Soon, malicious rumors were spreading that Barnum himself had taught the old woman all her George Washington stories and verse after verse of hymns. Some critics even accused him of forcing her to have all her teeth pulled. Barnum denied the accusations, and Levi Lyman even tried for a while to circulate a story that the body examined had not been the *real* Aunt Joice. Finally, Barnum decided that the furor would die down by itself and people would forget the whole Joice Heth controversy. The old woman was quietly buried back in Bethel, and Barnum, now an experienced showman, moved on to other projects.

While he was exhibiting Joice Heth in Albany, New York, Barnum enjoyed a show by Signor Antonio, a juggler with unusual talents like walking on stilts and balancing spinning china plates. Barnum offered Signor Antonio the chance to work for him. "I did not know exactly where I should use my protégé," Barnum admitted, "but I was certain that there was money in him." First Barnum had Antonio change his name to Signor Vivalla, because it sounded more foreign and exotic. Exotic things, Barnum was discovering, attracted bigger crowds. Barnum himself shared the stage with the juggler, assisting with props.

One evening in Philadelphia, while Signor Vivalla was onstage in front of a disappointingly small audience, there came a hiss from a corner of the theater. The critic was J. B. Roberts, a juggler with a circus that happened to be in town. Roberts wasn't impressed by Vivalla's tricks—why, he claimed, he could do much better himself.

Barnum sensed an opportunity for publicity. He printed an ad stating that Signor Vivalla would pay one thousand dollars to anyone who could come up onstage and copy his act, feat for feat. Roberts accepted the challenge, and arrived at the theater on the evening of the match. The hall was crowded to capacity.

As Roberts waited to go onstage, he had a confession to make. He admitted to Barnum that he *was* an accomplished juggler with many tricks Vivalla didn't know, but he really hadn't had much practice walking on stilts or spinning plates. Should he back out of the challenge? Barnum wouldn't hear

Signor Vivalla, a juggler whose specialty was spinning plates, toured the country with Barnum. (Courtesy of Somers Historical Society, Somers, New York)

of it, especially with a standing-room-only crowd watching.
He offered to hire Roberts as well as Vivalla, as long as the
two jugglers could convince the audience that they were rivals. Onstage, when Roberts's turn at spinning plates came
up, he failed. But he demonstrated a few fancy tricks new to
Vivalla, and offered a counterchallenge to be held the following week. The competition guaranteed another full house for
Barnum, and the challenges went on, back and forth, for
several weeks. If anyone in the audience suspected fraud, no
one complained: After all, they were seeing two champi-
onship jugglers at their best.

In 1836, Barnum joined up with Aaron Turner, who
owned a small circus. Together, they assembled a few performers, including Signor Vivalla, and went on tour. Circuses
were not the huge shows full of exotic animals and daring
stunts that we know today, though Barnum would later help
make them so. Turner's "circus" featured trick horseback
riders, a clown, Vivalla the juggler, and probably Barnum,
who had been teaching himself a growing array of magic
tricks.

Turner must have reminded Barnum of Grandfather Taylor, for he was another practical joker. One day, when the
circus was performing in Annapolis, Maryland, Barnum took
the opportunity to buy a new black suit, which he proudly
wore around town. The gossip of the day was about the
Reverend Mr. Avery, a minister in Rhode Island who had
been accused of a gruesome murder and found not guilty,
even though all the evidence was against him. Aaron Turner
began spreading the rumor that the stranger in the black suit
was the murderous minister, flaunting his freedom. First
Barnum noticed that people were looking at him strangely.
Then they were following him, and finally some were openly
shouting, "Murderer!" The situation got dangerous when a

group of angry men grabbed him, vowing to bring him to justice. Just then, Turner stepped in and explained that he'd been mistaken; Barnum was definitely *not* the Reverend Mr. Avery. He probably saved Barnum's life—but the new black suit was ruined. Barnum was furious, yet never forgot what his partner told him: "It was all for our good. Remember all we need to insure success is notoriety."

In Virginia, bad weather forced Turner to cancel his last day's shows and go on to the next stop a day early. The company, however, had paid in advance for three meals and lodgings at an inn, and the innkeeper refused to give them a refund for the uneaten food or unused rooms. At noon on the day they planned to leave town, all the circus people marched into the hotel dining room and demanded lunch. A half hour later they came back for supper. They went to their rooms for bed at one o'clock—but were back in the dining room at half past one for breakfast. By two o'clock in the afternoon, they were on the road, having used up a day's meals and rooms in two hours.

Not long afterward, Barnum and Turner decided to divide the circus between them and go their separate ways. Signor Vivalla continued on with Barnum, as did a black singer named Sandford and some others. Sandford disappeared one day, just before a performance—and Barnum found himself onstage that evening, disguised in makeup, singing a rousing set of African-American folk songs.

As the troupe traveled through Alabama and Georgia, they came upon a number of Cherokee Indians. Signor Vivalla was terrified of them, certain they'd attack while the circus camped for the night, as Indians did in all the stories he'd heard. One evening, some of Barnum's performers decided that, if Vivalla was so afraid of an Indian attack, they'd give him an Indian attack to remember. They dressed in buckskin and feathers and stole up on the juggler as he slept. Vivalla awoke to find himself being tied up as a band of "savages" rummaged through his belongings. In the morning, Vivalla was "rescued" and released, and his things were found and returned. The timid little juggler was convinced that he'd had an adventure, and that he was lucky to be alive.

After two intermittent years on the road, Barnum grew tired of traveling, and he disbanded his diminishing troupe of performers. It was time to return home to Charity and Caroline, who had been alone in New York and Bethel all that time. After months of excitement, what Barnum wanted was a quiet job that would let him invest the twenty-five hundred dollars he'd made with the circus and provide comfortably for his family. He advertised for a business partner and had some strange responses. Inventors invited him to their workshops to show him elaborate, impractical, and often fake machines. Pawnbrokers promised schemes to make him rich. One man approached Barnum, saying that he needed a partner to help him buy ink, dyes, and paper for his printing business. What he printed was counterfeit money.

Barnum finally settled on a partnership with a man named Proler. Together, they opened a factory that would manufacture ordinary products like cologne and waterproofing compound—as well as a miracle ointment guaranteed to cure baldness. Before Barnum knew what was happening, Proler had disappeared, taking his own money, *and* Barnum's.

Broke, Barnum returned to the job where he'd made his money. He assembled a group of performers and set out on another western tour. There was profit to be made in the circus life, and Barnum did so for a while, but it was keeping him from his family. Back in the city, however, jobs were tame in comparison—and Barnum tried everything from bartending to selling Bibles. There had to be some profitable line of work that would satisfy Barnum's craving for excitement, adventure, and entertainment, while keeping him close to home.

That was when Scudder's American Museum went on the market.

4
WONDERS OF THE WORLD

ENTERTAINMENT FOR THE COMMON PEOPLE WAS SCARCE IN America of the 1830s, and not very entertaining by today's standards. Many people attended lectures, but sitting for two hours listening to someone talking about the evils of alcohol or demonstrating a new invention is hardly what we would call fun. There were plays, but ministers preached against the unchristian morals portrayed in many dramas—even classics by Shakespeare—and criticized the dissipated lives of actors and actresses. Besides, in the dark, crowded aisles and boxes of many theaters lurked pickpockets and prostitutes plying their trades. No children or respectable ladies—and few real gentlemen—would set foot inside a theater. Some chose to ignore the ministers' warnings, so there were operas and ballets for the rich and well educated, and traveling musicians and crude sideshows for the less affluent and cultured. But the vast majority of Americans were ordinary people who attended a church service each Sunday where they were reminded that, if something was amusing, it was probably also sinful.

No one, however, had a bad word to say about education. Museums full of animal specimens or artifacts from other cultures were educational, and therefore permissible. They even served a religious purpose, some claimed, by displaying the wonders of God's creation, and emphasizing how "primitive" other cultures could be without the civilizing force of Christianity. If strolling through a museum was fun, too, there was no need to fear for one's soul; the amusement was outweighed by the learning experience. And because many museums contained inaccurately labeled, poorly organized, dusty, and badly preserved displays, they weren't *too* enjoyable.

That was the nature of the entertainment world when P. T. Barnum took control of Scudder's American Museum in 1840. Innovation was the key to success, Barnum knew, but he'd have to make his changes carefully and inoffensively. He wanted to continue to attract all those ordinary citizens who craved amusement but feared sin. He was also aware that it was nice to have visitors stop into the museum once— but to be truly successful he'd have to keep them coming back again and again.

To make the museum more appealing, Barnum began by redecorating, inside and out. He cleaned the dusty galleries, rearranged the displays, and got rid of the exhibits that were old and decaying. Then he used his growing contacts to scout out replacements.

When Barnum took over the museum, its exterior was very ordinary. There was nothing about the plain marble facade to hint that there were wonders to be seen within. So Barnum ordered painters to create a series of huge oval plaques, depicting all sorts of animals. For maximum surprise value, Barnum had all the paintings mounted in one night. By morning, the corner of Broadway and Ann was transformed, with the gigantic, brilliantly colored plaques mounted between each window of the building's fourth floor.

On the roof, among fluttering flags of all nations, Barnum installed a new invention that was brilliant in a different way. One night, the museum's corner was as bright as day beneath the glare of a Drummond light, a forerunner of the kinds of spotlights now used to promote things like grand openings of shopping centers. In Barnum's day, the Drummond light or limelight was a novelty, and he was the first to see how useful it could be as an advertising tool.

The museum had neighbors that attracted people, too. Nearby was Genin's, one of New York's most fashionable men's hat shops. All well-dressed men in the 1800s included hats in their wardrobes, and the Genin label was among the finest. Across the street from the museum was the studio of Mathew Brady, a pioneer in the new art of photography, who would build his reputation with pictures of the American Civil War. He sometimes used Barnum's latest attractions as subjects for his photographs.

Scudder's, like most museums at the time, featured a lecture hall. Throughout the day, scientists would demonstrate principles like magnetism to small audiences. Barnum, however, had bigger plans for his lecture hall. Almost as soon as the museum was his, Barnum closed the hall for extensive renovations. He had the small speaker's platform transformed into a real stage. He enlarged the audience area and installed comfortable seats for three thousand viewers.

When the "lecture hall" reopened, gone for the most part were the stuffy scientific speakers. What Barnum had created was a theater, one of the finest in New York City, and the safest. Precautions were taken against the sort of disreputable people who prowled the city's other theaters. Even the museum's employees were carefully screened: Barnum would not hire a person who indulged in alcohol. In his theater, Barnum guaranteed only the most wholesome plays, of the highest moral caliber, suitable for audiences of all ages. One of the most popular of the plays Barnum commissioned was a temperance melodrama, *The Drunkard*. A few years later, *Uncle Tom's Cabin* was another favorite. Here at last was a theater where respectable women could bring their children. The plays may have been oversanitized and free of anything offensive, but the theater in Barnum's American Museum opened drama up to a whole new audience.

The theater in the American Museum presented wholesome family dramas. (Gleason's Pictorial Drawing Room Companion, *January 29, 1853*)

Perhaps remembering those early-morning shoppers from his days as a store clerk, Barnum set unusual hours for his museum. Beginning on New Year's Day, 1842, it opened its doors at dawn. And there were enough visitors to keep it opening at that hour. Many tourists would walk through the museum galleries in the early morning before the city was awake, then set out for breakfast. The price of admission was also attractive to everyone: twenty-five cents, half that for children. Barnum, always a true businessman, once said that he disliked crowds—unless they were paying him a quarter a head.

One Saint Patrick's Day, the museum was literally crammed with visitors. Some had even brought lunches and were sitting on the floor around the exhibits, enjoying indoor picnics. People were lining up at the entrance, but were being asked to wait until the crowds inside eased up—and the crowds inside had no intention of leaving until they had seen *everything.* Twice. So Barnum cornered a painter who was doing some work around the museum and asked him to make and hang a new sign that would, he hoped, solve the problem. As the crowds milled about, they suddenly noticed a placard above a door. To the Egress, it read. Most of the people had no idea what an egress was, and assumed it was some rare animal, just arrived. They opened the door, walked down a flight of stairs—and found themselves outdoors, with a new word added to their vocabularies. An egress, of course, is an exit!

Barnum used every clever ploy he could dream up to attract crowds to his museum. One day, an unemployed man arrived in his office, hoping for a job. He got one—but it was a job that puzzled him. He was handed five bricks and told to walk around the block outside the museum, carefully and industriously laying down a brick at certain spots along the sidewalk. Each time he walked his circuit, he'd switch one brick for another. Most important, once each hour he'd enter the museum, appear to buy a ticket, walk through the galleries, then return to his bricklaying job. So many curious people followed the man around the sidewalk and into the museum, the police had to ask Barnum to stop his little scheme before the crowds created a serious disturbance.

The museum had a balcony overlooking Broadway, and Barnum hired a band to play there. He advertised it as "Music for the Millions": Since it was outdoors, it was free. A musician had to pass a special audition to get into Barnum's band, however. Barnum selected only the *worst* performers. The band was so bad, some people gladly paid a quarter to get into the museum, just to escape the noise! As Barnum would comment, what else did they expect for nothing?

What could a visitor expect to see for twenty-five cents in the five floors of displays that made up Barnum's American Museum?

In the basement was the physical plant—everything needed to keep the building heated and lit and properly maintained. And in later years, as Barnum expanded his collection of live animals, he used space in the basement for the largest creatures, including beluga whales. When *Moby-Dick,* a novel about the hunt for a white whale, was published in 1851, Barnum heard that, in the frigid waters of northern Canada, there *were* white whales: belugas. He was determined to capitalize on the popularity of the book and show the public *real* white whales. Traveling himself to Canada, he hired a whaling boat to capture a pair of animals and transport them to New York.

No one had ever studied beluga whales before, so Barnum had no idea how to care for them. Freshwater, not salt water, was pumped into a huge concrete tank in the museum's basement. The whales, of course, died in a few days. Thousands of people had come to see them in those few days, however, so Barnum requested another pair. While they were being captured, Barnum had the tank rebuilt, this time of slate and glass. Salt water right from New York harbor could be pumped into it. Besides whales, the basement tank sometimes held sharks, schools of tropical fish and sea horses, and even a hippopotamus, which Barnum advertised as a "behemoth," a gigantic creature described in the Bible. He hadn't forgotten how to appeal to the public's interest in religion and education as well as amusement.

Barnum caged all sorts of wild animals, from boas to baboons, in his museum. His indoor menagerie was not well cared for by modern zoo standards. And his attitude toward the animals, simply replacing specimens that died due to improper care, may seem cruel to us today. At the time, however, little was known about keeping wild animals in captivity—what they ate, how much space they needed, how they reproduced. As his menagerie grew to include expensive, exotic beasts, which he wanted to keep alive and happy for as long as possible, Barnum found himself in close contact with eminent scientists, such as naturalist Louis Agassiz. He also locked horns with defenders of animal rights such as ASPCA founder Henry Bergh. But in the early days of his collecting, Barnum simply tried to keep the animals alive long enough for many people to see them.

On the museum's ground floor, beyond the ticket office, was a large space devoted to a popular kind of nineteenth-century attraction: the panorama. Panoramas were paintings of famous events, drawn on very long rolls of canvas that nearly covered the walls of the display room. They gave the illusion of being in the middle of the event. Some popular panoramas depicted things like a trip across Europe, or Napoléon's funeral.

The second floor was a great favorite, more like a believe-it-or-not sideshow than a museum. Here were all sorts of odd and unusual things and people: two-headed calves, giants and dwarfs, and bearded ladies. On the same floor was a portrait gallery, alongside a display of wax figures of famous people. The most famous waxworks in the world was—and still is—Madame Tussaud's in London. For a while, Barnum seriously tried to buy Madame Tussaud's figures for his collection, but failed to make the deal.

Among the freaks and waxworks, near Ned the performing seal and a hall of distorting mirrors, was Barnum's own office. The showman *was* an attraction himself. One visitor bought a ticket to the museum, marched up to Barnum's office, looked in the door, and left satisfied. And when the Prince of Wales visited the museum on a trip to New York, he was disappointed to discover that Barnum was away. "We have missed the most interesting feature of the establishment," he complained.

The third and fourth floors were more what we would consider a traditional museum—although where Barnum was concerned, nothing was traditional. Here were mineral specimens and stuffed animals, Native American pots and blankets and a priceless collection of arms and artifacts from the American Revolution. Also on the third floor was the entrance to the lecture hall.

Anything having to do with the West, and especially with Indians, was automatically popular in the 1840s, because many people were leaving the East to settle on the frontier. Once, in addition to his collection of Native American artifacts, Barnum hired a band of live Indians from Iowa to stay at the museum. They set up their camp on the fourth floor, complete with tents and cooking fires. For a while, Barnum had them perform a daily war dance so realistic it struck fear into the hearts of viewers.

Even the most frightening show got boring after a while, though, so Barnum asked the Indians if they could put some variety into their act. They suggested a marriage dance, which Barnum felt was harmless enough. One prop they required was a brand-new blanket, which cost about ten dollars. Barnum provided a blanket, which the Indians used for the first dance. The next day, however, they refused to use the same blanket. The ceremony, they insisted, called for a *new* blanket each time it was performed. Barnum was finding his real Indians more complicated—and costly—to deal with than he'd anticipated.

Barnum's American Museum guaranteed five floors of sights and spectacles. (Gleason's Pictorial Drawing Room Companion, *January 29, 1853)*

Then, suddenly and unexpectedly, one of the most beautiful young Indian women died. Her grief-stricken companions dismantled their fourth-floor camp and returned to Iowa. Barnum, notorious for putting profits before people, simply set about finding exhibits to replace them.

Barnum liked the visitors his Indian attractions brought in, but he himself commented that he did not particularly like Indians, and his treatment of them was often far from respectful. Once, several important chiefs of western tribes were on the East Coast to meet with the president in Washington, D.C. Barnum arranged for the group to tour New York—but he also had them sit each day on the stage of the museum lecture hall as hundreds of viewers streamed past. The chiefs believed that the crowds were there to honor them—until an interpreter broke the news that they were actually on display, and people were paying to see them. Insulted, the chiefs returned to their people in the West.

The fifth floor of the museum housed Barnum's own vision of world harmony, the Happy Family. In one big enclosure roamed all sorts of specially trained small animals that normally would be enemies. Mice scurried unafraid among the paws of cats while birds of prey flew calmly above them.

Having seen all five floors of Barnum's American Museum, a visitor could finally sit down and enjoy an ice cream at a rooftop snack bar.

Sometimes the museum was the site of special events beyond its usual displays and exhibits. People loved pageants and contests as much in the 1800s as they do now, and Barnum saw his museum as the perfect location for such activities. He hosted shows featuring dogs, flowers, birds—even chickens. ("I am now in the midst of our poultry show," he wrote in a letter—"800 chickens in the museum. Gods! What a crowing!") He also held baby contests, with prizes for all sorts of exceptional babies—the cutest, the fattest, the quietest, the most identical twins and triplets. He offered a special $250 prize to any mother with a set of quadruplets, but none entered. At his first beautiful baby contest, he made the mistake of announcing the winner in front of the ninety-nine adoring mothers of the losers. The women mobbed the stage in angry indignation. In the future, winners were announced after the show, in writing.

Barnum was more interested in acquiring pieces for his museum and getting people to see them, than he was in identifying or cataloging his holdings. So there are no accurate figures of exactly how many individual things a visitor could see in the museum. One estimate put the size of its collection at 850,000 items.

Barnum's American Museum was not alone in inaccurately labeling its displays, or claiming that ordinary pieces were historically noteworthy. Once a clever journalist was touring the museum and interviewing Barnum. They were coming toward the collection of artifacts from the islands of Polynesia, and the journalist pretended to be impressed by its quality. Did Barnum, he wondered, own the very club that had killed the great explorer of the islands, Captain Cook? Certainly, Barnum replied; he even had documents to prove its authenticity. The journalist said he'd been sure that such a fine museum would have that valuable and historic piece—since several smaller museums he'd just visited had claimed to own it, too!

Vast and varied as Barnum's holdings were, he was always looking for spectacular additions. Some of his searches were successful, others weren't. In England, besides offering to buy Madame Tussaud's waxworks, he also expressed interest in the house where Shakespeare was born. The English weren't selling. Somehow, though, he *did* manage to acquire Queen

Victoria's state robes, which he sent to a fellow museum curator. To avoid a high tax, he shipped them back to America as secondhand clothing! With the gown came a note to the suspicious curator: "It is positively *true, on my honor, so help me God!* . . . I dare not tell *how* I got it—but I got it honestly & *paid for it.*"

Barnum had plenty more outrageous exhibit ideas that were impossible to carry out. He proposed buying Niagara Falls—just the American side. To make sure visitors on the Canadian side wouldn't be able to see his wonder for free, he would build a fence around it. The plan fell through. There was also talk of harnessing an iceberg from the North Pole to a boat and towing it into New York harbor for Barnum to display. When a sea serpent reportedly was sighted off the coast of Massachusetts, Barnum offered twenty thousand dollars to anyone who could deliver it to him. Although no one managed to find Barnum a sea serpent, one letter writer tried to convince the showman that he could catch the museum a live woolly mammoth—a creature that had been extinct for ten thousand years.

Barnum didn't jump at the prospect of a live mammoth. What *did* fascinate him, with indelible consequences, was a dead mermaid.

5

HUMBUGS

In 1817, a sea captain docked in Calcutta, India, bought a unique—and expensive—souvenir. He was so sure he'd found the ultimate curiosity, he gladly used six thousand dollars out of his ship's account to pay for it. The captain's souvenir was the preserved body of a mermaid. At least, that's what the man selling it claimed it was. It had been caught live in the net of a Japanese fisherman years before, he insisted.

The mermaid was about three feet long. She had a humanlike head with dark hair, skinny arms curled in the agony of a sea creature's suffocation, and dried-up little breasts. But below her waist all resemblance to a human being ended, for she had the dorsal fin and tail of a large fish. Being preserved, she was shriveled and dark brown, like a mummy. She didn't look much like most people's idea of a mermaid, but she *had* been dead awhile. And, despite her ugliness, she *was* astounding.

The captain's family back in Massachusetts did not share his enthusiasm for the souvenir when he returned home from his voyage. But he never gave up believing it was something special. When he died, one of his sons was aghast to discover that he'd inherited his father's monstrosity. All he wanted to do was to get rid of it. He sold it to Moses Kimball, who ran the Boston Museum. The Boston Museum was very much like Barnum's American Museum in New York, and Kimball was very much like Barnum, though less flamboyant. They both knew what kind of attraction guaranteed a good show, and they often shared exhibits. In 1842, Moses Kimball notified Barnum that he'd just come into possession of a genuine mermaid. Would Barnum, he wondered, be interested in showing it in New York?

The mermaid fascinated Barnum. He asked a naturalist to examine it and tell him if it was real. The scientist replied that it certainly *looked* natural: Skin and scales blended into each other so gradually, the creature couldn't have been sewn together, as he'd suspected. But, he added, it couldn't be real, for he didn't believe in mermaids. Barnum answered that, if this was a genuine mermaid just waiting to be put on display, he'd believe in mermaids.

Barnum knew that a curiosity like this needed a special advertising campaign. First he began to have letters and fake newspaper articles with datelines all around the country sent to New York papers, telling of a scientist, Dr. Griffin, who was transporting the body of a real mermaid to a London museum for study. As days went by and people became curious, it was revealed that Dr. Griffin would be stopping in New York. Local journalists flocked to his hotel room to see him, and of course, his mermaid.

"Dr. Griffin" was actually Barnum's trusted associate, Levi Lyman, and he had a story specially concocted for the press, a fantastic tale about the capture of a mermaid in the "Fejee" (Fiji) Islands. Just as Barnum had hoped, with all the publicity in the newspapers, New Yorkers were clamoring to see the mermaid themselves, while it was in their city. Reluctantly, "Dr. Griffin" agreed to postpone his trip to London and display the "Fejee Mermaid," for a very limited time, at that unparalleled showplace of scientific wonders, Barnum's American Museum.

Barnum had been sending illustrations of mermaids to the newspapers along with his articles about Dr. Griffin. The pictures showed human-sized women, fish-tailed but beautiful, nothing like the dried-up little creature in the museum. Then he ordered an eighteen-foot-long banner picturing a lovely mermaid, which he was planning to hang outside the museum while the exhibit was there. At that, Levi Lyman threatened to quit. He was the one who had to play the part of Dr. Griffin and actually show people the mermaid, he

The infamous Fejee Mermaid was hardly what audiences expected. (from Barnum's Own Story)

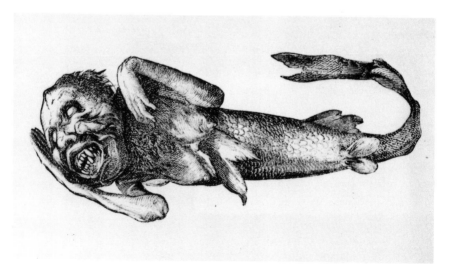

said—and he wasn't paid to deal with dissatisfied customers lured in by a deceitful banner. For one of the few times in his career, Barnum gave in.

Whatever they'd expected after the false advertising, audiences were fascinated by the Fejee Mermaid when the exhibit opened at dawn on August 8, 1842. But soon, Barnum's star exhibit was discovered to be a hoax that was, literally, "Made in Japan." Fake mermaids were turning up in museums and collections around the world. Careful, unbiased scientific examination proved that each mermaid was a piece of amazingly detailed Japanese craftsmanship: the upper part of a monkey sewn to the tail of a fish, its stitches imperceptible.

Although Barnum insisted that he himself really had believed that the mermaid was genuine, that even the scientists he'd consulted had been convinced, there was nothing he could say to erase the fact that he'd played a part in a hoax that had taken in thousands of people. The word spread that you couldn't always trust what you saw in Barnum's museum. When the Fejee Mermaid later traveled around the country, other curious items were displayed with it, including a stuffed platypus from Australia. This *is* a real animal, but for years people would continue to claim that it was manufactured, too: obviously a duck's bill sewn onto the body of a small mammal, with an opossum's pouch and an alligator's sharp claws added for effect. Mermaids like Barnum's—perhaps the Fejee Mermaid itself—are still in the collection of Harvard University's Peabody Museum of Archaeology and Ethnology—but now everyone knows that they are fakes.

Instead of hiding his head in shame, Barnum revealed a fact of human nature: Sometimes people *like* to be on the receiving end of a practical joke. Barnum is credited today with the line "There's a sucker born every minute." It's a clever statement, even if it is a bit cynical. But he probably never said it. His real words may have been something like, "People like to be humbugged." By *humbug* he meant a thing that is fake, packaged and advertised so cleverly that people could believe it was real—the classic wooden nutmeg. So Barnum would become a master at giving the public what it loved; he'd become a "Prince of Humbugs."

Sometimes Barnum, the Prince of Humbugs, was humbugged himself. He had agents all around the country, eyes open for new attractions and curiosities. A farmer once ap-

The rising young showman never said the famous words "There's a sucker born every minute"—but P. T. Barnum did *call himself the Prince of Humbugs. (from* Barnum's Own Story)

proached an agent with a squirming bag. In it, he said, was an irresistible find: a cherry-colored cat. The excited agent paid the man twenty-five dollars, then opened the bag. Inside was an ordinary cat, and it was indeed the color of cherries: *black* cherries. The story was so funny, Barnum reenacted the "deal" in the museum theater, then kept the cat, which eventually joined the ranks of the Happy Family on the fifth floor.

One of the first attractions in Barnum's museum, even before the Fejee Mermaid, had also been a humbug of sorts. The ads promised a realistic model of Niagara Falls, complete with "real water." Honeymooners who couldn't afford a trip to the Canadian border were among the curious who paid their quarter at the museum door to see the replica of the great natural wonder of the world. They expected to see hundreds of gallons of water thundering over rocky cliffs. The sight that greeted them was a small model, perfect in every detail of rock and tree, but barely eighteen inches high. "Real water" *did* pour down the falls, pumped over and over from a barrel below the model. Even the New York City water commissioners were fooled by the advertisements: They threatened to charge Barnum extra for the huge amount of water they thought he'd need to replicate Niagara Falls. He had to prove to them that the display used only a barrel of water a month! One magazine editor who viewed the tiny wonder commented, "Yes, it certainly is original. I never dreamed of such a thing. I never saw anything of the kind before since I was born,—and I hope with all my heart I never shall again!"

Barnum's American Museum included lots of natural curiosities, like calves with two heads and an immense hair ball from a pig. When Barnum acquired an unusual horse, he could have displayed it as just another curiosity. But he had bigger plans for it.

The little horse had been born without a mane, and even its skinny tail was hairless. Instead of a normal coat, it was covered with soft, curly, tan "wool," so Barnum called it a "Woolly Horse." The horse came from a very ordinary Indiana farm; Barnum knew he'd have to invent a much more exotic origin for it. He delayed putting the animal on display until the right opportunity arose. Meanwhile, he kept it hidden.

Around the same time, explorer John C. Frémont was on an expedition in the American West. The public had been following reports of his journeys with great interest—until suddenly, in 1844, he disappeared for several weeks in the dead of winter. It was a great relief to his fans when the charismatic explorer turned up alive and well.

Frémont was a celebrity. Anything connected with him was instantly popular. Barnum saw the chance to cash in on Frémont's popularity using the Woolly Horse. As he unveiled the strange little creature to the public, Barnum also revealed its invented "history," reportedly taken from a letter written by Frémont himself. One day when he was lost in the mountains, the explorer saw a bizarre camel-colored horse, covered with wool instead of hair, bounding away from him and his companions like an antelope. Frémont chased it and captured it, sending it east to the place where it would best be displayed, of course: Barnum's American Museum.

Frémont's father-in-law, Senator Thomas Hart Benton, was angry when he heard a story full of so many lies. But he couldn't prove that they *were* lies. Frémont had never written to Barnum telling him that he *had* seen a Woolly Horse, it was true—but he'd never written to say that he *hadn't* seen one, either. When the Woolly Horse quickly lost its crowd appeal, Barnum retired it to a comfortable life on a farm.

Another attraction that brought a piece of the American West to New York City was James C. "Grizzly" Adams. Adams was a hunter and trapper who had lived for many years in the Rocky Mountains, where he had assembled an amazing collection of animals: wolves, over twenty bears, and a sea lion named Old Neptune. In his rough buckskin clothes and a cap fashioned from a wolf's head, with a scraggly beard and long, unkempt hair, Adams was as unique as his menagerie. Barnum was thrilled to add the colorful mountain man and his animals to his shows.

Adams had come back east to his family, however, to die; he only wanted to perform with his bears a while longer to make enough money to provide for his wife. The huge grizzly bears Adams had trained over the years often playfully swatted at him. But they were so powerful, their swats could be deadly. Repeatedly, Adams's skull had been fractured, until a blow from a grizzly named General Frémont "had laid open his brain so that its workings were plainly visible." That was his condition when he came to work for P. T. Barnum.

Weakening day by day, Grizzly Adams nevertheless insisted on taking his animals on a final ten-week tour for an extra five hundred dollars, despite Barnum's warnings and protests. Just days after the tour ended, back home with his wife, Adams died from his terrible head injury. But his life ended with one last trick on P. T. Barnum. He'd asked the showman for a special suit of clothes to perform in, to keep as long as he needed it. Barnum had agreed to Adams's request. After Adams died, Barnum asked his widow to return the suit. She replied that her husband still needed it: He was buried in it. Adams did, however, leave his animals to the museum.

Not all of Barnum's humbugs were connected with the

museum. The infamous "Great Hoboken Buffalo Hunt" occurred on a small island in New Jersey. Barnum sponsored the event but kept his name and the museum's out of the advertising. Once again taking advantage of the public's fascination with anything having to do with the American West, Barnum had come into possession of a herd of fifteen young American bison, the thunderous beast of the plains. Rather than displaying them in his menagerie, he chose to stage a hunt on the island, free of charge except for a ferry fee and the price of refreshments. Twenty-four thousand people arrived to watch the spectacle, which was hardly the authentic hunt promised by posters. The young bison were nearly tame and stood for most of the time in a terrified huddle; the hunter was armed with only a rope lasso. When the bison finally stampeded, irritated by the jeering of the crowd, the situation got out of hand, and one spectator was killed falling from a tree he'd climbed to get out of the way. As crude and cruel as this seems today, Barnum and his audience considered it an afternoon's entertainment, popular enough for a repeat performance.

Buffalo entered Barnum's life again many years later. In 1870, Barnum and some friends were traveling through the American West. When they reached Kansas, they were invited to participate in a real buffalo hunt with a veteran soldier who had made a name for himself in the Civil War and who would die seven years later in the infamous Battle of the Little Bighorn: General George Armstrong Custer. Barnum surely recalled the Great Hoboken Buffalo Hunt from his early days as he and his companions shot down one beast after another from the vast herds on the open plain. This time, however, Barnum was appalled, not amused. The target was too easy. "During an exciting chase of a couple of hours," he wrote, "we slew twenty immense bull buffaloes, and might have killed as many more had we not considered it wanton butchery."

Barnum occasionally took things from his museum on the road in a sort of traveling exhibit and circus. One of his traveling shows included several live elephants. Not many people in America had ever seen an elephant—only a handful had come through the country in itinerant menageries—so the show was eagerly awaited. When Barnum's tour finally returned to New York, he decided to keep only one of the huge beasts. He sent that one up to his home in Bridgeport, Connecticut, which included a large piece of farmland bordering the railroad line. He also left unusual instructions for what to do with the animal. Each day, train travelers passing by Barnum's farm were astounded at the sight of a gigantic elephant, harnessed to a plow and driven by a man in Oriental dress, working in the fields. People began to contact Barnum, wondering if elephants were better at plowing than oxen or mules. No, Barnum replied—the elephant was advertising something very different: Anyone amazed by a plowing elephant would find further wonders in its owner's museum.

Learning the trade of showman, Barnum had met many other people in the profession, from circus manager Aaron Turner to magician Robert Houdin. They all gave the eager, promising young man the same advice: Perfect the art of advertising. He never forgot the value of that advice, and he passed it on. He once said that there was only one liquid a man could never use to excess: ink.

Barnum's posters were covered with words and pictures—far busier in layout than the roadside billboards we see today. Instead of plain, easy-to-read type, he chose letters with lots of curlicues and flourishes, so people would have to look closely. The pictures emphasized the most sensational things in the exhibits. And descriptions were exaggerated and "hyped," just short of being outright lies. Today there are laws regulating truth in advertising. For Barnum, the only truth in advertising was that publicity drew in people.

Barnum also discovered that, when it came to advertising, once was not enough. He developed a theory still valid today. According to Barnum, the first time a person passes a new poster or billboard, it's ignored. The second time, it's noticed; the third time, it's actually read. By the fourth pass, it's being thought about. Soon, it's discussed with other people. By the time a person has seen an ad six or seven times, he is ready to buy or do whatever is being advertised. So, when Barnum prepared publicity for something like the Fejee Mermaid, he slowly but surely flooded the newspapers with a continuous stream of letters and announcements, each guaranteed to be seen by more people, bring the attraction a little closer, and stir mere curiosity into excitement.

Barnum knew that what drew audiences were oddities, and even humbugs. But he never showed fakes for their own sake; no degree of advertising, he said, would give them lasting worth. What he really wanted to do was attract people through the doors of his museum, where there was much of real educational value—and sometimes a bit of overstretched advertising was the perfect draw.

There were some attractions, too, that didn't need overstretched advertising. One of those was the perpetually three-foot-high Tom Thumb.

INCREDIBLE PEOPLE

THE CURIOSITIES BARNUM DISPLAYED IN HIS MUSEUM WERE NOT just objects and animals. Some were human beings. Things had not changed much since 1835, when Barnum had exhibited Joice Heth. Audiences still flocked to reputable museums, and to disreputable sideshows, to see "freaks"—people who were, in some way, physically other than normal.

Barnum's collection of human oddities included giants over eight feet tall and midgets under three feet, women with bushy beards and albinos with snow white hair and pink eyes, people extraordinarily fat or thin, twins with bodies inseparably joined. Most of the day, Barnum's "freaks" sat in labeled spaces on the museum's second floor, more or less as they would in a sideshow. But there were also shows throughout the day, when some of Barnum's unusual people acted out roles onstage. For instance, a midget and a giant might reenact the biblical battle between David and Goliath.

Barnum was always watching for new unusual people for

his museum. Some his agents found. Some actually contacted him, asking for work. But Barnum himself found his most famous "freak," practically next door to his Connecticut home.

On a cold winter day in 1842, P. T. Barnum was traveling from Albany to New York City. He'd planned to take a ferry down the Hudson, but the river was frozen, so he found himself traveling by train instead. He decided to stop in Bridgeport, Connecticut, to visit with his half brother, Philo, who ran a hotel. Philo had exciting news for his museum-owning younger brother.

The Stratton family of Dutch Lane, Bridgeport, had two daughters, but it was their younger son that the whole neighborhood was talking about. Charley Stratton was five years old, an active and healthy child—and he was no bigger than he'd been as a baby of a few months! He was a midget, born with a defective pituitary gland, which affects normal growth. Unlike dwarfs, whose heads and limbs seem out of proportion with their small bodies, midgets look normal, only miniature. When Charley was born, he weighed a rather hefty nine pounds, two ounces. By the time he was five, he'd gained just six pounds, and was two feet tall. Barnum wanted to meet the incredible little boy himself. Through Philo, he made an appointment with the Strattons.

When Barnum arrived at the home of Sherwood and Cynthia Stratton, he was amazed at the sight of little Charley, dressed in a tiny blue velvet suit sewn for him by a neighbor. The showman was impressed by the boy's size, but the most popular museum people were also featured in acts; Barnum needed to know if Charley was as bright and articulate as he was tiny. At first, the child was a little afraid of the tall stranger and shyly refused to talk, but gradually he became more comfortable with Barnum. Charley Stratton, Barnum discovered, was not only remarkably small, he was also a delight!

At last, Barnum made the Strattons an offer. He'd hire Charley for a trial period of four weeks. During that time, he'd give the boy special tutoring in New York City—both a regular education and the sort of dramatic training he'd need for the museum. Cynthia Stratton could accompany her son. The payment at first was three dollars per week—not very much. At the end of the trial period, Barnum and the Strattons signed another contract, this time for just one year. Charley *was* only five, and midgets his age had been known to have sudden growth spurts that brought them to nearly normal size. Sometimes, too, they unexpectedly became ill and died. Barnum wasn't ready to take a long-term risk with Charley Stratton. His letters about the boy often included the phrase "if he lives."

Charley, of course, had to be properly advertised. When the Strattons saw the first posters announcing his appearance at Barnum's American Museum, they hardly recognized their son from the description. Remembering his successes in displaying things from abroad, Barnum decided that his new midget should be from a place farther away and more exotic than Bridgeport, Connecticut. Suddenly, Charley was English—just arrived from London, as a matter of fact. He was tiny for a five-year-old—but even tinier for a *twelve*-year-old. So Barnum added seven years to the boy's age. Finally, Charles Stratton was too ordinary a name in a gallery of odd people known as Colonel Goshen and Madame Clofullia. Barnum chose a name from legend for Charley: Tom Thumb. The original Tom Thumb was a knight of King Arthur's Round Table, a knight so small he rode a mouse rather than a horse, and met his death in battle with a spider. Barnum gave *his* Tom Thumb the rank of general rather than knight.

P. T. Barnum made midget Charles Stratton, better known as Tom Thumb, a celebrity. (Historical Collection, Bridgeport Public Library)

Barnum's small discovery was a natural show-off and quickly learned all sorts of dramatic scenes and funny songs and dances. He was an instant hit. Almost overnight, the question on everyone's lips was, "Have *you* seen Tom Thumb?"

Tom was so successful in Barnum's American Museum, the showman saw his opportunity to make a name for himself abroad. In 1844, P. T. Barnum and Tom Thumb, along with the Strattons and various tutors, set sail for England.

Things got off to a rocky start. Barnum had not arranged ahead of time for a hall where he could display Tom Thumb, and he had not scheduled any shows, so as soon as he arrived he had to find a respectable theater in unfamiliar Liverpool. Then, when Barnum asked an English showman how much he should charge for admission to see the midget, the reply was the usual price to see freaks in the area: a penny.

Fortunately, Barnum's museum business had acquainted him with all sorts of important people. He began to contact English friends; before long, Tom Thumb was performing at a good London hall, and visiting with minor royalty.

Some of these contacts had ties with Queen Victoria, and they let her know that England was enjoying a tiny visitor she might like to meet. On March 23, 1844, Tom Thumb's regular show was canceled: He had an audience with the queen.

Barnum and Tom were unsure of how to act around a queen and found the rules of proper etiquette bewildering. Tom Thumb relied heavily on his childish honesty and openness and got away with some otherwise unpardonable blunders. He called the queen and her court "ladies and gentlemen" as if they were an ordinary audience, then sang all eleven verses of "Yankee Doodle," a song from revolutionary war days that still gave English people a sour reminder of the loss of their former colonies.

Tom's worst mistake happened as he was leaving the royal chamber. He and Barnum had been told that it was impolite to turn their backs on the queen; when it was time to exit, they were supposed to back out of the room. Barnum was so much taller than Tom Thumb, the midget couldn't keep up with him. Not wanting to be left alone among intimidating royalty, Tom turned around and ran every few steps, then continued walking backward a few more paces, then turned and ran again. His running excited one of the queen's little lapdogs, which began to chase him. Running, backing up, and swinging a miniature cane at the barking dog, Tom Thumb finally reached the door.

Queen Victoria was not offended by the behavior of her small guest. On the contrary, she found him charming and amusing and invited him back to Buckingham Palace twice. She also gave him a number of valuable gifts. One present was a fine set of artist's tools. This was because he'd told the queen he was good at drawing. She didn't understand the show business pun, however; Tom didn't mean art, he meant drawing a crowd!

From England, Barnum and Tom Thumb traveled on to France, where they were also a popular attraction. Playwrights wrote comedies about "Tom Pouce," composers published songs, streetcorner vendors hawked souvenirs of the diminutive American. Princes and dukes showered expensive gifts upon their small visitor. When customs officials at the French-Belgian border saw the little general's elaborate traveling coach, they wondered whether he was royalty. The reply was, "He is Prince Charles Stratton, of the dukedom of Bridgeport, in the Kingdom of Connecticut."

Tom Thumb and Queen Victoria's dog caused a scene in his first audience with the monarch. (New York Public Library)

After three years of their highly profitable European tour, the pair returned to the United States. Thanks to the American Museum, but especially to Tom Thumb, gone were the days when Barnum, Charity, and baby Caroline had to live in a converted pool hall. The Barnum family had also grown. Besides Caroline, Barnum and Charity now had two other daughters: Helen, who was born in 1840, and Pauline, born in 1846. Another daughter, Frances, had died in 1844, when she was only two years old. The showman wanted a big, comfortable home in the country for Charity and the girls in addition to his brownstone on Fifth Avenue in New York City, and now he could easily afford it.

Barnum had fond memories of his native Connecticut, and still had strong family ties there. He began looking into property in an area that was then part of the town of Fairfield, although now it is in the city of Bridgeport: a large farm of seventeen acres, abutting the railroad to New York and just within sight of Long Island Sound. It was far enough from

New York City to be peaceful, but close enough to be convenient for a daily business commute. And Barnum insisted that the ozone levels in the fresh sea air were particularly healthful. He purchased the land and ordered construction to begin on his mansion, built "regardless of expense," which he named Iranistan. According to him, if not the dictionary, the name meant "Oriental villa." It's believed that he pronounced the name "Ih-ran-'is-tan," not "Eye-'ran-ih-stan" (or "Aaronstan," as Bridgeport natives say).

The quiet shoreline community had never seen anything quite like Iranistan. When he'd traveled to England, Barnum had been very impressed by George IV's Royal Pavilion by the beach at Brighton: an ornate construction of colorful domes, cupolas, and turrets with an Oriental flair. Barnum wanted the exterior of his mansion to be patterned after the Brighton palace.

The interior was every bit as lavish as the exterior. Ceiling and wall panels were painted with elaborate scenes. Orange satin draped the walls of Barnum's personal study. The cupola, which contained an astronomical telescope, also housed a comfortable sitting room whose windows were made of diamond-shaped panes of multicolored glass. One of Iranistan's main attractions was a newfangled invention Barnum was especially excited about: a bathroom shower with cold *and* hot running water.

Nearly overnight, a team of landscapers transformed the bare fields that had surrounded the mansion into cool lawns and shady glades of full-grown oaks and elms. Barnum refused to look at spindly saplings year after year until they grew into trees; he demanded his landscape ready-made. Tame elk roamed about the parklike grounds—within sight of the plowing elephant. From Iranistan's stables, Barnum drove his magnificent black carriage horse, Bucephalus.

Above: *Barnum's first Bridgeport mansion was the fanciful Iranistan. (Historical Collection, Bridgeport Public Library)*. Below: *Barnum's magnificent black carriage horse was named Bucephalus. (Barnum Museum, Bridgeport)*

Tom Thumb, too, began to enjoy the comfortable life of a rich celebrity. Although he stopped formally touring with P. T. Barnum in 1848, the two remained close friends, and he was a frequent guest at Iranistan, which celebrated its official housewarming on November 14 of that year. Like his friend Barnum, he built a home for himself and his family in Bridgeport, overlooking Long Island Sound. It was a home comfortable for both midgets and normal-sized people: All the doorknobs were especially low; and while some rooms were furnished with ordinary tables and chairs, others were full of custom-made, midget-sized furniture. He had miniature coaches made, just twenty inches high and pulled by a team of perfectly matched twenty-eight-inch Shetland ponies. As he grew older, Tom learned to sail the waters of Long Island Sound and owned his own racing yacht. He raised prize racehorses. He had everything a successful young show business personality could possibly want, except a wife. Where, he wondered, would he find a woman enough like him to consider marrying?

With the rousing success of Tom Thumb, Barnum was alert to the audience appeal of other midgets. He hired one young man whose name, George Washington Morrison Nutt, was bigger than he was, at just twenty-nine inches. Barnum dubbed him Commodore Nutt. The commodore drove about in a tiny pony-drawn carriage shaped like a walnut that Barnum ordered for him.

Some time after this, Barnum made the acquaintance of Miss Lavinia Warren Bump of Massachusetts. She was a schoolteacher, although at thirty-two inches in height she was shorter than most of her third-grade students. She was less enthusiastic about being part of Barnum's museum than Tom Thumb and Commodore Nutt had been, but she finally agreed to join the show.

From the moment he met Lavinia, Tom Thumb was determined to make her his wife. For a while, he and Commodore Nutt were in fierce competition for the hand of the pretty midget, a competition that once even led to a fistfight. Lavinia, however, settled the matter: One evening when they were guests in Barnum's home, she accepted Tom Thumb's proposal.

The two were married on February 10, 1863, in New York City. Nutt and Lavinia's sister Minnie, also a midget, made up the wedding party. Barnum was pressed with demands to turn the wedding into a media event, maybe even selling tickets. But Tom Thumb and Lavinia were more to Barnum than his employees and star attractions: They were his friends. He felt responsible for having brought the couple together, and he respected their privacy. The unusual wedding was appropriately dignified.

Some time after the wedding, photographs began to appear of Lavinia holding a baby. This was a hoax; she and Tom Thumb never had children. Tragically, Lavinia's sister Minnie married a man of nearly normal height; she and her baby died in childbirth.

As they grew older, Tom and Lavinia appeared in their own shows, only occasionally contracting with Barnum. Although they were no longer business associates, the midgets and the showman remained close friends all their lives. Tom Thumb died in 1883 at the age of forty-five, and was buried in Mountain Grove Cemetery in his native Bridgeport. Lavinia married Count Magri, another midget and actor, a few years later. When she died, however, she was buried beside her beloved Tom Thumb with the simple epitaph HIS WIFE.

Barnum's other human oddities never attained the same degree of popularity as Tom Thumb, but they were definitely unusual people in their own right. Chang and Eng, for in-

Tom Thumb and Lavinia Warren were married in 1863, with Commodore Nutt and Minnie Warren as attendants. (Historical Collection, Bridgeport Public Library)

stance, gave the world the term "Siamese twins," meaning babies born joined at some part of their bodies. They were the sons of a Chinese family living in Thailand, then known as Siam. A firm but flexible armlike ligament, about five and one-half inches long, united the twins at the chest. They spent

Chang and Eng were the original "Siamese twins." (Historical Collection, Bridgeport Public Library)

most of their lives in exhibits like Barnum's, hoping to earn enough money to finance the operation that might separate them. They were adults when Barnum hired them, and not easy to get along with. Eng, the right-hand twin, was rather quiet and reserved; Chang on the left, however, loved parties, food, and drink. Barnum finally arranged a European tour for the twins—partly to show them there, partly to allow them to see some special surgeons. The doctors' report was conclusive: Chang and Eng might have a head, two arms, and two legs apiece, but they shared a liver and bloodstream. Separation was impossible. They would live out their lives joined by five and one-half inches of muscle. This did not prevent them from marrying two sisters, taking the American surname Bunker, and raising a total of twenty-one children.

Another of Barnum's human attractions was named by Charles Dickens. During a visit to New York, the author dropped into Barnum's American Museum, which was a favorite stop for any tourist. Dickens, however, enjoyed a special tour guided by Barnum himself. On the second floor, he stared at one of the "freaks" in amazement, and finally asked, "What is it?" The name stuck; for years afterward, Barnum billed William Henry Johnson, or Zip, as the "What Is It?" Johnson was a black man born with a skull smaller and narrower than normal, which rose to a point; people like him were commonly called "pinheads." He was probably mentally retarded, but he was clever enough to know that he could make far more money in shows like Barnum's than he could in the few other jobs open to people like him. He played a variety of "primitive" characters like the "missing link" between animals and humans. Many of Barnum's exhibits toured Europe at some point in their careers, and most were as popular there as they were in the United States. The What Is It?, however, did not appeal to cultured Continental audiences.

Rudolph Lucasie and his family were African albinos. Racially, they were black, but their skin was pale, their hair—even the children's—was white and curly, and their eyes were pink. Along with the Lucasie family, Barnum also displayed what he called "Leopard People": African-Americans with a condition called vitiligo that left their skin mottled and patched brown and white.

While the Lucasies were famous for their white hair, Madame Clofullia was famous for her abundant hair—in an unusual place. As a young girl in Switzerland, she had begun to sprout whiskers. By the time she was an adult, she had a full, bushy beard. Her infant son was as heavily bearded as his mother. People insisted that Madame Clofullia must be a man dressed in a woman's clothing; she finally had to agree to a physical examination to prove that she *was* a woman.

In contrast to midgets like Tom Thumb and Commodore Nutt, Barnum hired giants like Monsieur Bihin, seven feet, eight inches tall, and Colonel Goshen, eight foot two. The two men were great rivals, always fighting—until Barnum told them that, if they *must* fight, they could at least do it onstage and attract a paying audience. Not all the giants were men; Anna Swan, from Nova Scotia, Canada, was nearly eight feet tall and weighed 413 pounds.

In Barnum's hall of human oddities, visitors could also see S. K. G. Nellis, a man born without arms who could handle a knife and fork, a bow and arrow, even a cello, using only his agile feet. They wondered at a man whose entire body was covered with tattoos. They were amazed at four-year-olds who weighed over two hundred pounds, or at people so thin they resembled walking skeletons.

Today we would consider a display like Barnum's second floor degrading—although we are still fascinated by record books that list the oldest, the tallest, the heaviest. In the 1800s, however, people with severe deformities or disabilities didn't have many options in life. Most employers then wouldn't dream of hiring someone so unusual that customers would stare or feel uncomfortable. Few jobs would accommodate someone of abnormal size or with special needs. For a midget like Lavinia Warren to become a schoolteacher was a rare occurrence. Many of these people ended up in institutions. If they were determined to make a living, it was generally as a member of a sideshow. And, as displays of "freaks" went, Barnum's American Museum was one of the more humane.

People were used to Barnum's advertising the most weird and sensational aspects of humanity, often with plenty of exaggeration. So they found it hard to believe when he announced a legitimate artistic venture: the American tour of a human nightingale.

7

NIGHTINGALE

FOR HIS USUAL AUDIENCES, BARNUM PROVIDED ENTERTAIN-
ments like staged buffalo hunts, woolly horses, and morally
impeccable plays. When *he* wanted to be entertained, however, his tastes were very different. Barnum enjoyed quality
theater and classical music, and frequently attended operas,
ballets, and symphony concerts (tastes Charity Barnum did
not always share). There, he began to hear about a young
singer from Sweden, Jenny Lind, who was being praised
across Europe as one of the finest sopranos who had ever
lived. Her nickname, given to her by the British magazine
Punch, was the Swedish Nightingale.

Despite his hoaxes and humbugs, Barnum's goal—besides making money, of course—was to educate people while
entertaining them. Ordinary people in the United States had
few opportunities to hear opera performed by really fine
singers, and most had very little interest in that sort of music.
Barnum had a plan that would introduce huge crowds of
eager listeners to quality music—and, if it worked, he'd be

a far, far richer man besides. And Jenny Lind, a woman Barnum had never actually heard sing, was the key to his plan.

Johanna Maria Lind, nicknamed Jenny, was an illegitimate child raised in a very prudish, restrictive household. When Jenny was nine years old, a dancer with the Royal Opera House in Stockholm heard the little girl singing to her cat. Her voice was so promising, the Royal Theater School offered to accept Jenny as a student free of charge. For years, Jenny devoted herself to her music, perfecting her high, pure soprano voice. Jenny sang in her first opera at the age of sixteen, and trained with the finest vocal teachers on the Continent. She was soon the darling of sophisticated Europe, starring in all the most famous operas. Composers like Felix Mendelssohn wrote music especially for her; storyteller Hans Christian Andersen, in love with the young singer although she scorned his affection, was inspired by her to write "The Emperor's Nightingale."

But Jenny was unhappy with the life surrounding an opera star. Because of the strict moral training of her childhood, she couldn't help feeling uncomfortable singing in many operas that told melodramatic stories of illicit love affairs. Before she was thirty years old, she announced that she wanted to retire from the opera stage. She would, however, continue to sing carefully selected programs, mainly folk songs and sacred works, donating her earnings to various charities.

That was when she met a man named John Hall Wilton. He'd been authorized by America's foremost showman, P. T. Barnum, to negotiate an American concert tour for the Swedish Nightingale—if she was interested.

Although Barnum didn't say so, Jenny Lind fit perfectly into his philosophy of entertainment. She had a reputation for being generous, pure, moral, and religious. Her voice was unique, superlative, widely acclaimed. She sang music in her concerts that was of high quality overall, but included songs that would appeal to wide ranges of taste and preference. And she was, Barnum had heard, thinking about a trip to America.

He was not the first to approach the young singer with the idea of an American concert tour. His competitors warned Jenny that Barnum was an unscrupulous, money-hungry showman, more famous for fake mermaids and midgets than for legitimate art. With Barnum, they claimed, she'd be seen as an exhibit, not a singer. But the man intrigued her anyway. The letter Mr. Wilton handed her was on Barnum's personal stationery, with a fancy letterhead depicting Iranistan. A man who could build a house like that, Jenny reasoned, knew how to make money—and it couldn't *all* be from hoaxes. Also, Barnum was the only businessman who was offering solid cash up front, not just promises of payment. As soon as Jenny agreed to the deal, he said, he'd deposit all the money due to her in a special account in a bank in London. There would be no danger of her traveling and singing, then having to cope with a manager who couldn't or wouldn't pay.

Jenny told Wilton that she would accept P. T. Barnum as her tour manager. She chose several companions, including two fine musicians to perform with her: Julius Benedict, a pianist and composer; and Giovanni Belletti, an operatic baritone. And, she informed Barnum, she could be in America as early as September of 1850.

Barnum was thrilled at the news, but a little apprehensive about the date. He had only six months to book concert halls around the East Coast all the way to the Mississippi River, and to prepare publicity. The publicity was desperately needed, as Barnum soon discovered. Jenny Lind might have

Barnum arranged renowned soprano Jenny Lind's concert tour of America—before he'd ever heard her sing. (Historical Collection, Bridgeport Public Library)

been the talk of Europe, but in America she was unknown. Barnum mentioned her name to a train conductor one day; the man thought she was some sort of dancer.

Barnum engineered a wave of celebrity frenzy that rivaled a reaction to a rock star today. He was paying nearly thirty reporters to write for him at various papers, so the press was inundated with notices about the singer's arrival. Before long, even people who had no clear idea of just who Jenny Lind was or what kind of music she sang were clamoring for a chance to see her. To miss being part of her audience, the notices implied, would be like turning one's back on a rare appearance of Halley's comet!

Today sports figures have sneakers named for them; television shows have spin-offs ranging from toys to breakfast cereals. In 1850, if you wanted your product to sell, you implied that Jenny Lind used it, or at least endorsed it. America found itself inundated by Jenny Lind hats, Jenny Lind shawls, Jenny Lind stoves, Jenny Lind cigars (despite the fact that she *hated* cigar smoke), even Jenny Lind mule bridles!

As Barnum knew from the baby, dog, and poultry shows at his museum, people love to enter contests. So he announced that, at her first New York City concert, Jenny Lind would sing a new song written especially for her American tour. Amateur poets were invited to enter a competition to provide the new song's lyrics; a cash prize of two hundred dollars would also be awarded. The winning poem would then be set to music by Julius Benedict. There were 732 entries. The winning poet was Bayard Taylor, who wrote "Greeting to America." As in any contest, there was grumbling afterward from the losers, but the competition served the purpose for which it was intended: It stirred up excitement.

When Jenny Lind arrived at the port of New York on

September 1, 1850, she was greeted by banners and a cheering crowd of thirty thousand spectators. She could hardly leave the ship without being crushed. She believed the crowd was spontaneous; actually, Barnum had been in constant touch with the ship, demanding the exact time it would dock, so he could spread the news and ensure an enthusiastic audience. He continued to do the same thing throughout the tour, always keeping his plots from Jenny. When she later toured without Barnum as her manager, she was puzzled by the empty train stations and lack of fanfare at her arrival.

Crowds greeted Jenny Lind at her arrival in New York harbor, and at every stop along the tour—courtesy of P. T. Barnum. (Historical Collection, Bridgeport Public Library)

Tripler Hall in New York City, where Jenny's first concerts had been scheduled, was still under construction when she arrived. So the site was switched to Castle Garden, set on an island in New York harbor. The first and best tickets, Barnum announced, would not be sold outright. Instead, they'd be auctioned to the highest bidders. People knew that the high bid for something as special as Jenny Lind's first performance would be publicized nationally and would make someone famous, so bidding was vigorous. The highest bid for that concert—$225—came from John Genin, the hat merchant whose shop neighbored Barnum's museum. Genin's fine hats had always been popular, but after the auction, a Genin hat was a real mark of distinction.

To prevent charges of unfairness, Barnum would not let any of his employees bid on seats at the auctions; they had to wait until ordinary tickets were sold. So, when Charity Barnum told her husband that she'd like to attend one of the New York concerts, Barnum had to buy a ticket for his own wife!

Barnum also auctioned off the best tickets for Jenny's concerts in large cities like Boston. Genin's bid was low compared to the $650 offered by a Colonel Ross in Providence, Rhode Island—who didn't even attend the concert. But Jenny began to object to the ticket auctions. While she was glad to make so much money, which she planned to donate to charities including a special school in Sweden, she was unhappy that tickets were often too expensive for working people to afford. In Boston, she heard a story about a girl who'd bought a three-dollar ticket to one of her concerts. She'd commented that, although three dollars represented a week's wages, it was worth it to hear Jenny Lind sing. Jenny managed to track her down and send her a twenty-dollar gold piece. Finally, Jenny persuaded Barnum to set reasonable prices for all tickets. He also made rules that would prevent anyone from buying large numbers of cheap tickets, later selling them for much more. Unscrupulous "scalpers" were operating even then!

To deal with the crowds he expected at the concerts, Barnum devised a system to guide people to their proper seats quickly and easily. All seats were assigned. Tickets were banded with one of four colors. The hall was then divided into four sections, and the seats in each area were marked with the same colors. Even the ushers carried colored wands. So a person with a blue ticket knew to follow a blue usher to a seat in the blue section. People who could not afford a seat could buy a "promenade" ticket and stand through the concert.

When the great Jenny Lind finally stepped onto the Castle Garden stage in her white gown, carrying a spray of white flowers, some people among the five thousand in the audience seemed disappointed. The only pictures they had seen of her were copies of sketches or paintings, not photographs, and artists of the time were careful to flatter their famous subjects and make them attractive. The young woman people saw in Castle Garden looked nothing like her portraits. She was tiny, with a round, plain, rather peasantlike face and an awkward nose. Then, however, she began to sing in her high, clear voice, and people quickly forgot that she was not a stunning beauty.

While the concert included orchestral works and solo pieces sung by Giovanni Belletti, Jenny Lind was the star her fans had come to see, and she thrilled them with a selection of operatic arias, duets, and folk songs. Audiences especially liked some of the Swedish songs, in which Jenny mimicked mountain echoes and bird trills. She concluded the concert, as promised, with Bayard Taylor's "Greeting to America."

Jenny's New York concerts were presented at Castle Garden. (Historical Collection, Bridgeport Public Library)

After the audience cheered the young performer back onstage for her triumphant bows, they demanded Barnum, too—and he proudly received his applause at Jenny's side.

Jenny's program varied slightly from time to time, but she and Barnum quickly discovered that a purely classical concert simply wasn't as popular as a mix. Barnum had convinced vast numbers of ordinary Americans that they desperately wanted to hear an acclaimed Swedish opera singer. But he could not convince them that they wanted to hear two hours of classical music.

Most of the audiences were respectful and orderly. Still, as long as there have been concerts by international stars, there have been gate-crashers and rowdy elements. At Castle Garden, some people tried to sneak in by boat and scale the walls. Elsewhere, a stable down the street from the concert hall sold "seats" for fifty cents, in the hopes that Jenny Lind's voice would carry that far. One of the halls Barnum booked in Boston became so suffocatingly hot during the concert, people began breaking windows for air. A riot nearly ensued. The audience in Madison, Indiana, though, was appreciative in spite of the "auditorium": The largest hall Barnum could find was a hog butcher's shed. Men always outnumbered women at Jenny Lind's American concerts, sometimes by as much as ten to one! Maybe it was because of the appeal of the unmarried young songstress, or maybe it was because there was always some fear of danger when big crowds assembled.

When Jenny's tour began to travel south, Barnum's eighteen-year-old daughter, Caroline, was one of the group's traveling companions. Since she was seen so often with her father, sometimes she was mistaken for the famous singer herself. In Baltimore, Caroline attended church with a friend, who invited her to sit with the choir and sing. The rumor spread that it was none other than Jenny Lind singing that morning in the church, and people praised the heavenly voice of the young stranger. Barnum, amused, remarked afterward that he'd never noticed anything special about his daughter's voice.

Sometimes Barnum had Caroline impersonate Jenny on purpose. In several railroad stations, the crowds mobbed the train and refused to move until they caught a glimpse of Jenny Lind. So Caroline put on one of Jenny's outfits, covered her face with a shawl or a bonnet, and elbowed her way through Jenny's cheering fans on her father's arm. The people followed them, clamoring for a song or an autograph, while the real Jenny Lind quietly slipped out of the train, unnoticed. For her part, Caroline didn't like her famous traveling companion very much; she considered the singer spoiled and conceited.

In Havana, Cuba, Jenny met with unreceptive audiences and other problems, so Barnum canceled her concerts and the troupe took a needed vacation. Jenny found a little house for rent that was far more comfortable than the hotel, and she passed the time in the garden, where Barnum joined her to play games of catch with a big rubber ball.

In Havana, Barnum also ran into an old friend from his early days as a showman: Signor Vivalla. A stroke had left the acrobat and juggler nearly paralyzed, but he was still performing with a trained dog, making a very poor living for himself. As soon as Jenny Lind heard about him, she insisted on meeting him and his dog, and on helping him in some way. He was soon a guest in the little Cuban villa. Signor Vivalla mentioned that he would love to see his native Italy again, and Jenny was ready to pay for the trip—but it was too late. A few months later, she and Barnum received word that the old performer had died.

Jenny's troupe was under a lot of pressure, traveling and performing on a tight schedule, not always in the best conditions. And while the public saw her as sweet and angelic, Barnum had to deal with the stubborn, temperamental side of Jenny Lind's artistic, perfectionist personality. Luckily, he had a talent for keeping the mood light throughout the tour. On April Fools' Day, Barnum played an elaborate trick. He had fake telegrams delivered simultaneously to everyone in the entourage. Musicians received incredible job offers. One man whose wife was pregnant heard that she'd just given birth—to twins! Entire neighborhoods burned to the ground, whole families were waiting at the tour's next stop. None of the messages was true, of course. When people began to meet to share their news, they realized that the Prince of Humbugs had struck again.

Barnum and Lind had originally agreed to produce 150 concerts around the country. Jenny's business advisers, however, still didn't trust Barnum, in spite of the huge audiences pouring in. They kept recommending that Jenny revise her contract so she could sing fewer concerts, even if she'd lose some money in the deal. She finally agreed. She wanted a rest from all the traveling and a pace of one concert every day for nine months. Barnum, too, had not spent time at home with his family for far too long; he was as weary of touring as the musicians. Jenny Lind sang her final concert under P. T. Barnum's management—their ninety-third—on June 9, 1851, back in New York City.

Jenny Lind stayed in America for a while, setting up her own arrangements for an additional forty-eight concerts, at a much less hectic pace. But her venture without Barnum was not as successful; she lacked his showman's instincts with the public. Also, during the tour she married Otto Goldschmidt, who had replaced Julius Benedict as her pianist. Her fans didn't think the talented but rather dull Goldschmidt was good enough for the angelic Jenny. And she lost some of her audience appeal once she got married.

Almost everyone who ever worked with P. T. Barnum remained his friend for life, and Jenny Lind was no exception. While there were things about her American concert tour she would have done differently, Jenny had to admit that Barnum's arrangements had been stunningly successful and profitable, and she was grateful.

Just as important, P. T. Barnum had proved to the world that he was good at more than humbug.

"A MAN'S HOME…"

P. T. BARNUM HAD MADE HIS MILLIONS BY BEING ONE OF THE
brashest, most flamboyant personalities of his day. But while
Barnum *seemed* to want to make everything about himself
newsworthy, there was much about his family life, Charity,
and his daughters that he kept private, too. There were never
any colorful magazine exposés of life behind the opulent walls
of Iranistan, and Barnum himself did nothing to draw attention to his family.

For all of her life, Charity stayed in the shadow of her
husband's overpowering public image. Sometimes she traveled with him, but she tended to be a nervous worrier. She
was also more of a traditional, conservative New England
"Puritan," and didn't enjoy things like ballet and opera as
much as her husband did. She was especially shocked by the
dancers, with their filmy costumes and bared legs. So she
generally remained at home while her outgoing, jovial husband roamed the globe. Periodically there were rumors of
infidelity, but despite his frequent travels, Barnum seems to

have been devoted to the woman he met in the thunderstorm.

If Barnum said little in public about Charity, he said even less about Caroline, Helen, and Pauline, how they were brought up, or what they did as children in their father's huge mansion.

By 1848, when the family moved into Iranistan, Barnum had spent the better part of the past thirteen years on the road. He had often been away on his travels during family crises. He was in Europe when baby Frances died, and when Pauline was born. Finally, he had a place to put down roots, a place where he could escape the public eye and enjoy his family and his friends. "I count these two years—1848 and 1849—" he said, "among the happiest of my life."

Iranistan was perfect for entertaining friends—but Barnum's hospitality had limits. He had embraced the temperance movement and would not drink or serve alcohol. As a young man, Barnum had liked a good time. His letters to friends during his trip to Europe with Tom Thumb had been full of the praises of fine French wines. Once he even helped crush the grapes with his bare feet! So when he began to build his mansion with entertaining in mind, Barnum included a well-stocked wine cellar. His mother-in-law, who sometimes spent extended visits with the Barnums, cautioned him against becoming too fond of drink. But he ignored her warnings until one of his many tours brought him to a convention near Saratoga, New York. Many of the men there had been drinking, and Barnum was disgusted by the condition and behavior of people he otherwise respected. Then he heard a minister deliver a powerful lecture on temperance. Not long afterward, Barnum returned to his new home, dragged the bottles up from his impressive, expensive wine cellar, and emptied them onto the lawn. He also signed a temperance pledge, vowing never to touch alcohol again.

Helen, Pauline, and Caroline Barnum grew up in Iranistan. (Barnum Museum, Bridgeport)

Some of the worldly people Barnum dealt with, including Jenny Lind, were puzzled when he insisted on drinking a toast with plain water. But he had never been a man to change his convictions because of what others thought. In fact, he took every opportunity to make witty but passionate speeches against drinking. At one of his lectures, a man asked Barnum how liquor affected a man most, internally or externally. Barnum quickly replied, "*E*-ternally." After he embraced the temperance movement, Barnum even made his employees, especially at the museum, sign its pledge. Drinking alcohol was grounds for dismissal. He knew smoking was bad for his health, too, but continued to enjoy good cigars until he was in his fifties.

He might be private concerning his family, but Barnum loved publicity, seeing his own name and activities in print. In 1854, he created an uproar with the first of many editions of his autobiography. In it, he revealed the secrets behind Joice Heth and the Fejee Mermaid, and was openly delighted in having humbugged so many people. Readers were not sure what to make of such honesty—whether to respect the man for being so clever, or hate him because he repeatedly and unrepentantly fooled the public. But the autobiography, dedicated "To the Universal Yankee Nation, of which I am proud to be one," was certainly popular. For a while, it was the second-most-read book in America, with only the Bible ahead of it.

It was inevitable that the author of the immensely popular autobiography would meet that other famous Connecticut writer, Mark Twain. Twain had built a home in Hartford, sixty miles to the north—a home as unusual and as typical of its owner as Barnum's Iranistan. Long before he actually met Barnum, he wrote a funny essay about the absurd things he and the showman might do to publicize a comet that would soon be appearing. Barnum, who loved to be written about, good or bad, serious or silly, enjoyed the piece. He began a correspondence with Twain. A tentative friendship developed; the Barnums and the Twains occasionally invited each other to their respective Connecticut homes. But the relationship *was* tentative, mainly because of what Barnum expected from it. Again and again in his letters, Barnum asked Twain if he would consider writing a series of publicity pieces for him. The combination of two incredible talents, he reasoned, would surely lead to profitable results for both of them. Twain, however, was apparently insulted that his "friend" wanted to use him in that way. When Barnum persisted, he became annoyed. The correspondence and visits dwindled, then stopped as time went on, and the promising friendship finally cooled and died.

P. T. Barnum was by far the most famous person living in the Bridgeport area—a national celebrity. And celebrities tend to be seen as experts on everything, with valuable ideas and opinions—even on things they know little about. Barnum was also immensely wealthy due to the success of his museum, and along with wealth come power and prestige. Soon, Barnum found himself invited to run for all sorts of public offices.

Because his property was, technically, a farm, he was elected president of the Fairfield County Agricultural Society in 1848. He admitted in his first speech that he knew nothing about farming. He even made a joke about his plowing elephant. He might not have been the best farmer in the organization, but he certainly was the most colorful president it ever had.

Barnum's speeches may have emphasized what he *didn't* know, but they did so in a way that made people enjoy listening. Before long, he was being encouraged to run for higher offices. In 1865, the United States was divided by the Civil War. Barnum was in his fifties, and too old to fight, but he paid for four soldiers to fight for the Union in his name, something many older, wealthy Northerners did. He'd been a Democrat all his adult life, but President Lincoln was a Republican, and Barnum agreed with the policies of the president. He switched parties. Almost immediately, he was elected to the Connecticut State Legislature, representing Fairfield. Because of his membership in the Agricultural Society, he became chairman of the Agriculture Committee. Barnum served a total of two terms in the state legislature in the 1860s. In 1877, he was elected again to Connecticut's General Assembly, chairing the Temperance Committee.

Barnum was not just a figurehead representative; he had strong, sometimes unpopular, views, and he spoke up for what he believed. One of his landmark speeches demanded the right to vote for Connecticut's black citizens. Another of his projects involved undermining the grip that the powerful railroad business held on government. Laws always seemed to favor the railroad men. Barnum fought the injustice, disregarding the number of enemies he made in doing so.

Barnum insisted that he didn't want to seek public office, but in 1867 he found himself nominated to run for a seat in the United States Congress. He waged a solid campaign, but lost to his Democratic opponent—in fact, a distant cousin of his, William H. Barnum.

In 1888, P. T. Barnum had the opportunity to run for the highest office in the land: president of the United States. Because of his stand on temperance, the Prohibition party wanted him to be its candidate. A presidential campaign by a man like Barnum, with advertising savvy and an unabashed ability to hoodwink and humbug, would surely have gone down in history—and, if he had won, his term would have been, if nothing else, interesting. Barnum, however, turned down the offer.

In 1875, Barnum was elected Bridgeport's mayor. Critics contend that during his one term, he was away on showman's business too often to really manage the city's affairs, especially for a salary of only five hundred dollars per year. But when Barnum left office, Bridgeport's streets were brightly lit by newly installed gaslights, and the city's water supply had improved, due to his efforts as mayor.

His contributions to the city were philanthropic as well as political. He established a scholarship to be given to a high school student who excelled, predictably, in public speaking, and was instrumental in the foundation of the Bridgeport Public Library in 1882. The first borrower's card it issued was, of course, Barnum's. A developing city needed a hospital; Barnum's funding made one possible. He even served as president of a bank.

Barnum was also concerned with the beauty of his community. Bridgeport borders Long Island Sound, but when Barnum first arrived there few residents could enjoy the ocean: The land along the sound was privately owned and jealously guarded. There wasn't even a road where people could ride or stroll by the water. Barnum bought up a chunk of oceanfront property and had it landscaped by Frederick Law Olmsted, who designed Central Park in New York City (and Barnum's private property as well). Calling the area Seaside Park, Barnum then gave it to the city of Bridgeport. With his own money and contributions from others, he contracted for a spacious avenue that would run through the city directly down to the new park and Long Island Sound.

In 1855, however, most of these accomplishments still lay far in the future. Barnum was probably thinking of himself as a sort of King Midas: Everything he touched seemed to turn to gold. He had big plans for himself, and for Bridgeport, and failure was not part of his experience. He had no idea what a minefield of disasters lay ahead.

FIRE AND RUIN

In the early 1850s, Barnum was full of ideas to improve Bridgeport, which he accurately predicted would one day be Connecticut's largest city. One of his plans was to develop some unused land across the Pequonnock River from his property. He wanted to create a model community, East Bridgeport, with carefully laid out residential streets of reasonably priced homes whose residents would work in the modern, productive factories Barnum hoped to attract. He even proposed a strict moral code for the community: Anyone who intended to live in East Bridgeport would have to sign the temperance pledge.

Barnum was relatively successful finding people interested in living in East Bridgeport. He had less luck attracting businesses to the area. There was just one factory of high quality, which manufactured coaches. Then he heard about the Jerome Clock Company: the enterprise that would spell his downfall.

When the disastrous affair was over, neither Barnum nor the Jerome family could say for certain who had approached whom first. Either way, Barnum entered into an agreement with the New Haven, Connecticut, clock manufacturers. He would lend them some money they claimed they needed to get them through a slow season. In return, they would relocate their factory to East Bridgeport. Barnum took a quick look at their records, saw that they were known for quality craftsmanship and generosity to the community, and thought he had found an ideal business for East Bridgeport. He should have checked into the Jerome Clock Company's finances more carefully—but he must have believed that his days of dealing with people who sold sacks of potatoes by the pound (with a few rocks added) were long past.

The Jerome Clock Company asked Barnum for advance after advance on its loan, and he responded with check after check, believing the money was going toward improvements, and that it was all being repaid. He was lax in keeping track of exactly how much he'd given. The factory also kept delaying its move to Bridgeport. Then, suddenly, the Jerome Clock Company declared bankruptcy, and Barnum discovered how much of his money it had swindled, and where his funds had really gone. The company had lied about why it had needed the money: It had been using it to try to get itself out of debt, all the while sinking deeper. And it was P. T. Barnum's signature on all the promissory notes the Jerome Clock Company's creditors began to produce, demanding immediate payment. Altogether, the dept amounted to about half a million dollars—far more than Barnum was able to pay at once. He tried to keep up with the debts for a while, but finally he, too, was forced to declare himself bankrupt in 1855.

Life changed overnight for the Barnums. Luckily, much of Barnum's money and property were in Charity's name, and couldn't be touched by her husband's creditors. Barnum always acknowledged how much he owed to Charity during that difficult time: He and his family avoided becoming totally destitute because of her.

The Barnums moved out of Iranistan and into rented rooms in New York City, sometimes staying with friends on Long Island. Barnum prepared to sell his beloved mansion. His real estate agent had no idea who would dream of buying it—but he agreed to see what he could do.

When he went bankrupt, P. T. Barnum was forty-five years old. He had enjoyed his years of unsurpassed success and prosperity. Most men his age would not have considered trying to rebuild their fortunes and regain their glory. Some of Barnum's friends advised him to accept the disaster and quietly retire on Charity's money. Others, including Tom Thumb, offered to aid the fallen showman with donations. But Barnum rejected all the well-intentioned offers of assistance. And his Yankee pride refused to let him admit defeat and leave a debt outstanding. He would, he vowed, pay back every cent he owed with his own earnings and regain his standing in his community and in the business world. He considered his bankruptcy an omen, a sign that he had begun to care too much about money. Now he would have a second chance. Incredibly, in the midst of those dark days he was able to say, "All praise to Him for permitting me always to look upon the bright side of things."

Not long before the failure of the clock company, Barnum had sold the American Museum to its managers, John Greenwood, Jr., and Henry D. Butler, so he could concentrate more on business than showmanship. The mortgage was taken over by the bank to go toward Barnum's debts. Secretly, however, Barnum continued to work with the museum, planning exhibits and presenting shows to earn a little much-needed cash, careful never to use his name. Luck was with Barnum as he planned his clandestine exhibits. While he was staying on Long Island, a black whale washed up on the beach, dead. It was Barnum's first showpiece on the long road back to success. Soon afterward, he organized an English tour for some American actors who had achieved popularity on the museum's stage; Tom Thumb, and even that old hoax, the Fejee Mermaid, joined them.

While Barnum was in England, he was asked to deliver a lecture. He chose as his subject the successful businessman. He called the speech "The Art of Money-Getting"—although he joked that lately he was better at *losing* money than at making it. The lecture was popular, and before long Barnum was in demand as a speaker all around the country. He was again making rather than losing money.

Barnum worked as cleverly and as energetically as he had as a young man trying to pay for the American Museum. Now, though, he had the advantage of being a famous personality. His efforts paid off: By 1860, five years after disaster struck, P. T. Barnum had repaid nearly every cent he owed from the Jerome Clock Company failure. And it was a happy day when Greenwood and Butler could announce that the American Museum was once again *Barnum's* American Museum. The showman was well on his way to rebuilding his fortune. But more problems lay ahead.

Fire had been a bad omen for P. T. Barnum for a long time. Early in his career, he'd invested ten thousand dollars in a company that made a new invention, a sort of fire extinguisher. The contraption, however, didn't work, and didn't sell. And in 1852, just before his daughter Caroline's wedding to David W. Thompson, there was a small fire at Iranistan. But these incidents were minor in comparison to what was to come.

In 1857, after Iranistan had stood empty for many

months with no potential buyers, the Barnums decided to move back in. But first, the house needed some repairs after being neglected for so long. One evening, a spark smoldered, probably from a workman carelessly smoking near a sofa in the glassed-in cupola. The mansion was soon engulfed in flames; by the morning of December 18, 1857, it was a charred ruin. The loss was doubly serious for the Barnums. Iranistan was worth hundreds of thousands of dollars—but it was insured for only twenty-eight thousand. So Barnum lost much more than his home when Iranistan burned to the ground. Some furniture was salvaged, but even the things that were saved were damaged by the fire. The onion-domed marvel of Bridgeport was gone forever. The land was sold to Elias Howe of sewing machine fame, but he died before he could build anything on it.

After recovering from his bankruptcy, Barnum built another spacious mansion in town, near his daughter Caroline's new home. He called his second mansion Lindencroft. But it was very different from Iranistan. The old home had been the fanciful, flamboyant dream of a young man displaying for all the world what his wealth could buy. Lindencroft was the stately manor of an established businessman. It was rich and comfortable without being conspicuous. Yet it still bore the mark of Barnum's personality: For instance, the house was equipped with a burglar alarm that set off a barrage of fireworks when triggered.

No Civil War battles were fought anywhere near Barnum's property. But the war affected the American Museum in a bizarre and fiery way. A small group of Confederate sympathizers in the North hatched a plot to set off firebombs at important places in New York City. The men were badly organized, however. Most of the bombs wouldn't explode, and the conspirators began to back out of the plot. One of

After Iranistan burned to the ground, Barnum built Lindencroft with its startling burglar alarm. (Historical Collection, Bridgeport Public Library)

them, seeing his moment of glory slipping away, ducked into the American Museum with his firebomb. In frantic desperation, he threw it at the main staircase—and it turned out to be the only one of the bombs that worked. A small fire started, but was rapidly brought under control without causing any major damage. Barnum was shaken—but relieved.

By 1865, the war was over, and P. T. Barnum was back on his feet. The indignity of his financial disaster was nearly forgotten. On the morning of July 13, he was sitting in the House of Representatives in Hartford, serving his first term in the state legislature. It was his turn to speak on the subject of the railroad monopolies. Suddenly, a messenger dropped a note onto his desk. Barnum read the note, folded it, finished his speech, then excused himself. The American Museum in New York, he explained, had just burned to the ground.

A spark in the basement, probably in the boiler room,

had started the fire, which spread rapidly. Fortunately, no human lives were lost, since few people were in the building at the time. All the human oddities were safely evacuated from the second floor. Anna Swan, the eight-foot giantess, was overcome by the heat; firefighters needed a derrick to hoist her out a window to the ground.

The animals in the museum, however, were not as lucky. Cages were opened, and smaller creatures like birds and snakes were able to escape. But large or fierce animals could not simply be set free to roam the city, and some were too frightened to leave their pens. The whale tank was smashed ro release gallons of water in a vain attempt to put out the blaze. The whales died a horrible death, as did the big cats, hippos, and other valuable animals. Priceless relics, too, were destroyed. While workers managed to save the safe from the office and a few slightly melted waxwork figures, one of the finest collections of revolutionary war memorabilia ever assembled went up in flames, as did countless Native American and Pacific artifacts. And again, the collection was insured for only a fraction of its worth.

Once more, Barnum's friends urged him to accept the fire as a sign that it was time to retire. Barnum, however, saw opportunity amid the ruins. He said that the United States *needed* a large, comprehensive museum, and there was no one in the country more qualified to run it than P. T. Barnum.

With so much of his collection destroyed in the fire, Barnum needed new exhibits if he wanted to open another museum. He sent letters to prominent people around the world, politicians and statesmen, scientists and collectors, asking for contributions from their own libraries, memorabilia, and souvenirs. These, Barnum explained, would become part of a national museum that would be open to the public free of charge. It was a noble idea, uncharacteristic of the moneymaking Barnum people knew. And, of course, there was a catch. Next door to the free museum with its mineral specimens and papers of ex-presidents would be another, separate museum, also run by Barnum, which would charge visitors a quarter to see freaks and oddities, mummies and live animals—all the things that had made the American Museum such a success but would be inappropriate in the sedate neighboring collection. It's not hard to guess which museum would be more popular. Barnum soon abandoned his idea of a national museum, especially since the new Smithsonian Institution in Washington, D.C., was already beginning to serve a similar purpose.

Barnum had been in the business long enough to know whom to contact when he needed African masks or Egyptian mummies or Asian elephants. Before long, expeditions around the world had assembled enough items to fill a new museum. Barnum occupied a building on Broadway between Spring and Prince streets; and, on November 13, 1865, Barnum's New American Museum opened its doors.

The new museum was a popular attraction. But in a way, comparing it to its predecessor was like comparing Lindencroft to Iranistan. Much of the novelty had worn off: Gone were the limelights on the roof, the gaudy plaques of animals on the facade, the atrocious band—all that had been outrageous and flashy and flamboyant. The museum, even Barnum-style, had grown into an acceptable form of public entertainment. Barnum no longer had to prove the educational value of his amusements.

On the bitter cold winter morning of March 3, 1868, Barnum and Charity were eating breakfast. An item in the morning newspaper caught Charity's attention: Barnum's museum, it said, had burned. "Of course it did," her husband replied, and went on with his breakfast. As Charity read on, however, it became clear that disaster had just struck twice. Barnum's New American Museum had caught fire on the previous evening. Once again, while there was an appalling loss of animal life, no people died in the blaze. Firefighters did what they could, but it was so cold, the water from their hoses froze even as it extinguished the flames. The next morning, the museum was a sadly picturesque ice castle. And once again, the insurance Barnum had taken out on the museum would not even begin to cover the monetary loss.

Fire was not yet finished with P. T. Barnum. Barnum, however, was nearly finished with museums. A museum was fine for people who lived near it, or for tourists. But countless people—in America and around the world—couldn't make the trip. And they would enjoy seeing oddities and artifacts and shows, too. If the people can't come to the museum, Barnum reasoned, the museum could go to the people. And so began the phase of his life for which P. T. Barnum remains most famous.

THE CIRCUS IS COMING!

THE CIRCUS IS PROBABLY WHAT MOST PEOPLE TODAY ASSOCIATE with P. T. Barnum. But in fact, he did not get seriously involved with the circus until late in his life, long after he had made his reputation as a museum manager. As a young man, of course, he'd toured with Aaron Turner, and he'd had his own small troupes, but without a menagerie of animals to accompany them, those productions were more like traveling vaudeville shows than circuses. That, however, would change, and P. T. Barnum would be part of the reason.

In 1870, Barnum was sixty years old. He'd survived the destruction by fire of his two successful museums. He'd remade his fortune after bankruptcy and the loss of his beloved Iranistan. His friends suggested that now, at last, it was time to retire. The ever-active mind of P. T. Barnum, however, had other plans.

Barnum made the acquaintance of two experienced showmen: Dan Castello, a former clown, and W. C. Coup, a savvy circus manager. The three agreed to a partnership, forming

"P. T. Barnum's Museum, Menagerie, and Circus." Barnum's name alone was a useful addition to the venture. People knew that, if something was produced by P. T. Barnum, it would be out of the ordinary. Besides, Barnum was an expert at locating unusual animals for the menagerie, or curiosities for the museum tent.

Coup was a genius in his own way. His specialty was coordinating the hundreds of people and animals involved in a circus, making sure that everyone was where he belonged, on time. So Coup was a natural person to invent the idea of a circus with different acts going on simultaneously in multiple rings; he was used to juggling several complicated schedules at the same time!

Before Coup, circus performances took place in one ring in the center of a big tent. The ring was always thirteen meters in diameter. The size was standardized so that horses trained in a thirteen-meter ring could be traded from circus to circus. But the people farthest from the center ring in the big tent couldn't see the action very well; they might get bored by even the funniest or most exciting act if they couldn't see it. Since the ring couldn't be made larger, Coup suggested that there should be *two* thirteen-meter rings, with different kinds of acts running at the same time. Everyone in the audience would then be close enough to one ring or the other to enjoy the show. A few years later, the circus of P. T. Barnum and his associates featured *three* rings—then three rings and a track around the outer perimeter for racing events. Audiences hardly knew which way to turn!

Coup had another brilliant management idea. He and his partners had in mind a circus on a grand scale. Their company brought along not only performers and animals, but also its own cooks and seamstresses, blacksmiths and leatherworkers. Five hundred workers and horses were needed to man and pull the lumbering wagons that moved the circus, slowly, from one town to the next. The troupe couldn't go very far overnight, so show locations were close together, and those locations were often very small towns. Even if the town's entire population turned out, attendance figures would hardly make the circus worth the effort. Coup, however, announced that now Barnum's circus would be transported by train instead of wagons. Less time would be wasted moving from place to place; more time could be spent performing. And the circus could concentrate on big, central cities instead of isolated small towns.

Barnum, experienced in disaster, liked the idea of steel railroad cars: "a new invention, something that can't be smashed up." (He spoke too soon. On every tour, there was at least one serious train accident.) Three engines were needed to haul the sixty freight cars packed with equipment and animals and the six passenger cars full of performers and staff. But the circus was able to arrive in a city in the early hours of the morning, parade its colorful wagons and columns of rare giraffes and gigantic elephants down Main Street at 8:00 A.M., present two or three shows, and be on its way to its next destination by evening.

Under Barnum, the circus turned into a flamboyant, extravagant spectacle. His immense tents held twenty thousand spectators—and they were generally full. In the three inner rings, acrobats balanced on high wires, graceful ladies and trick goats rode splendid horses, the daring Zazel the Human Cannonball (actually Rosa M. Richter) exploded from the mouth of a cannon, and costumed bears and elephants danced. The outer track was full of wild activity—perhaps a chariot competition, or silly races between ostriches or camels with monkeys as jockeys.

Other circus shows were more like pageants, featuring

casts of hundreds of people and animals. They portrayed events: an attack on an Indian camp, an authentic English stag hunt, or an epic biblical story. Anyone who'd had enough of all that action could step into one of several connected tents to look at the collection of wild animals, the sideshows of human oddities, or the museumlike collection featuring a cross section of a redwood tree so big it took two hundred children to encircle it and wax figures of famous people.

Outdoors there might be even more happening. For a while, Barnum planned to be the first to fly a hot-air balloon across the Atlantic Ocean. An experienced balloon pilot, Professor Donaldson, traveled with Barnum's circus, talking about his unusual sport and giving people rides, until one fateful day in Chicago. Donaldson and a newspaper reporter had set off on a routine ascent in the professor's balloon when a strong wind came up, sending the craft far off course. Apparently it was wrecked in Lake Michigan, where the reporter's body was later found. Donaldson and the balloon, however, were never recovered.

Barnum's vast operation was not free from problems, but he was as proud of his circus as he had been of his museums. This was entertainment for families, and Barnum tolerated no misbehavior on the part of his circus employees. Most traveling shows and performers had bad reputations: Circus people, the puritanical public asserted, had loose morals. Barnum, however, discouraged drinking and sexual misconduct among his workers. Even as a young man with Aaron Turner's circus, Barnum had been sensititve to the prejudice against showmen. Several times, he'd attended church services where the theme of the minister's sermon was vice— with the visiting circus as an example. Offended, Barnum would stand up and demand an opportunity to tell the congregation about showmen who were God-fearing, honest, churchgoing people—like him.

As Barnum grew older, establishing himself firmly in the circus business, he also changed his nickname. As a young showman, he'd been proud of the title Prince of Humbugs. Now, instead, he wanted to be known as The Children's Friend. There is a story, which may or may not be true, about Barnum's compassion for children. When his circus arrived in Cleveland, Ohio, he heard about a boy who desperately wanted to see the show, but was seriously ill and confined to his room. According to the story, Barnum changed the route of the circus's morning parade so it would pass by the sick boy's house. He even had some of the animals perform tricks in the boy's yard.

There are some children's adventure and animal books supposedly written by Barnum himself. But he also looked for opportunities to have other authors write about his circus. He contacted popular children's magazines like *Golden Days for Boys and Girls* with an attractive offer. They could send one of their writers on tour with Barnum's circus, to live with the troupe and see firsthand what circus life was like. It was irresistible material for any publication for youngsters.

On the other hand was the P. T. Barnum who wanted to eliminate something children today automatically think of when they hear the word *circus*. Upset about the sale of refreshments at his shows, he wrote, "I *think* also I will never again permit candy and lemonade to be peddled, but furnish *free* ice water for my patrons." What would the circus be without cotton candy and peanuts!

Not everyone believed in P. T. Barnum's compassionate, child-loving image. A number of very young children performed with the circus. Barnum was charged with violations of child labor laws. He won those cases, proving that these children were not being harmed or exploited, but actually thrived on performing.

He also ran into problems with Henry Bergh, founder of the ASPCA. Their first encounter involved the New American Museum and its collection of live snakes. Bergh was aghast that the snakes were fed live rabbits; he was even more furious when he learned that visitors could watch at feeding time. Calling upon the expertise of noted naturalists, Barnum proved to Bergh that the snakes' natural diet consisted of living creatures; they would not eat previously killed meat. But he did agree to feed the snakes without an audience watching.

Some years later, Bergh was upset by one of Barnum's circus animal acts. Salamander, a highly trained trick horse, did stunts involving fire, such as leaping through a burning hoop. Bergh feared the horse was in danger. Barnum replied that the fire was produced by safe chemicals, and that Salamander was protected by being thoroughly wet down before the trick. Bergh persisted in his complaints. Finally, one night at the circus, Barnum himself, followed by a line of clowns and one of Bergh's assistants, leaped through Salamander's burning hoop. Not a single hair was singed. Bergh had to admit that Salamander's dramatic trick was far less deadly than it looked.

Despite their disagreements, Barnum and Bergh grew to respect and even like each other. They went about it in different ways and for different reasons, but both men wanted to ensure that animals were properly cared for and understood. The beasts in Barnum's menagerie were often the first of their kind in the United States, sometimes animals that had never before been kept in captivity. He seemed to give barely a second's thought to an animal—or a human performer—that died and had to be replaced. But his successes, like keeping captive giraffes alive longer than the previous record of two years, provided valuable examples for future zoos. Barnum helped found the Bridgeport chapter of the ASPCA, and donated money for a fountain in Sea-side Park commemorating his friendly antagonist, Henry Bergh.

American circuses in Barnum's day didn't perform much during the cold winter months, except for an occasional tour of southern states. Barnum needed a place where his animals could spend the winter—and, of course, they could draw an audience while they were there. He obtained a rickety old building in New York City, named it the Hippotheatron, and proceeded to move in his giraffes and rhinos, polar bears and sea lions, big cats and ostriches. Again and again, the fire marshal warned him that the building was unsafe. They were warnings he should have heeded. Barnum's nemesis, fire, struck again. In a half hour, the Hippotheatron burned to the ground; once again, most of the valuable animals, except for two elephants and a camel, were killed in the fierce blaze. If he grieved for the animals' painful deaths, he never showed it. Always the businessman, Barnum simply began the process of ordering a new menagerie from his suppliers around the world. Soon he was presenting shows in the Hippodrome, at Fourth and Madison in New York City.

The year 1876 was a special one for the United States. It was the Centennial, the nation's hundredth birthday. And Barnum, of course, had spectacular plans for a yearlong celebration. For thirty minutes starting at the stroke of midnight as January 1, 1876, began, every church bell in Bridgeport would ring in the New Year. What followed, in every town Barnum's circus visited across the United States, would be "a real old-fashioned Yankee-Doodle, Hail-Columbia Fourth-of-July celebration every day." The circus parade featured men in revolutionary war costumes, including actors portraying George Washington and the Marquis de Lafayette mounted on white horses. Fifers and drummers marched, not far from what must have been a very irritated live eagle, secured to a perch on a float and hauled along the parade route. Choruses of hundreds of singers were assembled to thunder out patriotic songs. Each day ended with a stunning fireworks show. Appropriately, Barnum called his entertainment "The Greatest Show on Earth."

Barnum went through several partners, including circus pioneer Isaac Van Amburgh, but it was *his* name that blazed across the advertisements and brought in the crowds. Not long after his triumphant Centennial celebration, Barnum met his match in circus business savvy: competitor James A. Bailey.

Bailey, an owner of International Allied Shows, had a happy announcement to make. One of his circus's elephants, Hebe, had just given birth. The baby, named Columbia, was the world's first elephant born in captivity. When Barnum heard about Columbia, he contacted Bailey and offered him one hundred thousand dollars for the baby. Bailey not only refused to sell, he began to use Barnum's hefty offer in his advertising. For once, someone owned something that the great P. T. Barnum wanted and couldn't have.

Barnum was too much of an old Nutmegger to be offended by his rival's clever ploy. In fact, he was impressed by the audacity of the young showman, forty years his junior. It was a move worthy of Barnum himself! In 1880, Barnum made Bailey another offer, a far more important one. He proposed that they merge their circuses, including Bailey's current associate, James L. Hutchinson, in the partnership. That was the beginning of the Barnum and Bailey Circus, as it was officially called by 1887.

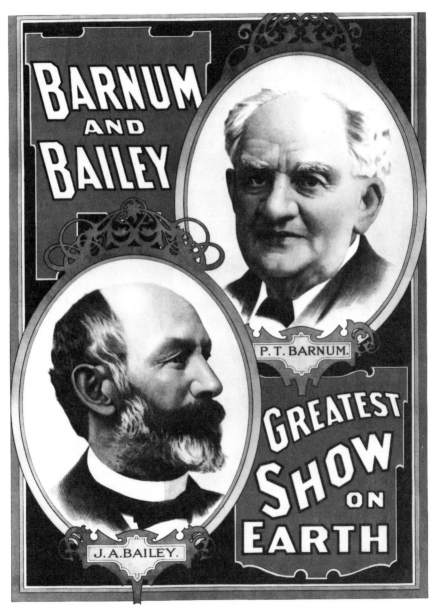

P. T. Barnum and James A. Bailey made their circus "The Greatest Show on Earth."
(Barnum Museum, Bridgeport, and Ringling Bros.-Barnum & Bailey Combined Shows, Inc.)

Barnum nearly didn't get a chance to enjoy his new partnership. During the winter of 1880, he fell seriously ill with a stomach ailment. He'd always been a big man, six feet and well over 200 pounds. As his illness progressed, he lost 75 pounds. Churches near his Bridgeport home held services to pray for his recovery. After many months facing death, Barnum slowly regained his health. But his old vitality was diminished. Once he'd delighted in traveling about the country for months at a time. Now, he informed his partners, he would spend time with the circus when it was convenient, but he would be conducting much more of his business from home.

The show that opened in 1881 was every bit as big as its name: "P. T. Barnum's Greatest Show on Earth, Howe's Great London Circus and Sanger's Royal British Menagerie." The entire entourage paraded down Broadway, where people paid for window space to watch the spectacle, all the way to Madison Square Garden, whose three rings and two stages guaranteed nonstop thrills.

Scouting about again for suitable winter quarters, Barnum decided to store the equipment and stable the animals where he could keep an eye on them: in Bridgeport. On the warmer and sunnier winter days, the animal handlers would parade the elephants and giraffes and camels down Iranistan Avenue to Sea-side Park. To the delight (and, probably, surprise) of city residents also enjoying the pleasant day, the animals would play and bathe in the waters of Long Island Sound before heading back to their stalls. And at the Bridgeport winter quarters a second baby elephant was born. It was named, appropriately, Baby Bridgeport.

The disaster that now seemed nearly inevitable for P. T. Barnum struck on the evening of November 20, 1887. A fire began in the winter quarters, rapidly consuming valuable

The winter quarters of the circus were in Bridgeport, Connecticut. (Historical Collection, Bridgeport Public Library)

costumes and elaborate wagons—and, again, killing most of the helpless animals. Some of the elephants succeeded in escaping their burning stalls, and charged down the familiar avenue to Sea-side Park. The water should have spelled safety, but the weather was already cold, and one elephant who plunged into the sound later died of exposure. An old lion, Nimrod, also escaped only to meet an unfortunate end. He took shelter in a farmer's barn, making a convenient meal of a sheep. Angry and frightened, the farmer shot the lion on the spot.

After surveying the disaster, Barnum went to consult with Bailey. He found his partner at his desk in the early-morning hours, writing and sealing letters. Bailey calmly explained that he had already finished securing a new menagerie.

The winter quarters were rebuilt and remained in Bridgeport until as recently as 1927.

Many years before, the Prince of Wales had left Barnum's American Museum disappointed because he hadn't seen its greatest attraction: Barnum. At Jenny Lind's concerts, the audience had demanded a bow from Barnum, too. At each circus performance, the audience wanted Barnum again. To comply, whenever he was with the tour, the seventy-year-old showman would ride his horse-drawn coach around the ring a few times, then shout, "You came to see Barnum? Well, I'm Barnum." The crowds, of course, went wild.

11

ONE BIG ELEPHANT

BARNUM'S CIRCUS INCLUDED ALL SORTS OF EXCITING ATTRAC-tions, but for three years its star was the spectacular Jumbo, the largest elephant in captivity—perhaps the largest elephant alive at the time.

As a youngster, Jumbo had been quite ordinary. When he was captured in East Africa at the age of four, he was less than four feet tall. He was shipped to a zoo in Paris in 1861, where he was a rather unimpressive specimen. The Royal Zoological Gardens in London was looking for a new elephant; Paris thought little of parting with young Jumbo, trading him for a rhinoceros.

It was at the London Zoo that Jumbo began to grow larger and larger, eventually approaching an astounding height of eleven feet, with an agile trunk seven feet long. Originally, his name had not had any special meaning; it had simply been "African-sounding." As people heard about the big elephant in London, however, *Jumbo* began to mean "exceptionally huge."

Such a gigantic beast could be terrifying if he were wild and untamable, but Jumbo was a sociable giant. He enjoyed the zoo's visitors, especially the children who brought him treats of peanuts and sweet rolls. (It was less publicized that Jumbo was as fond of beer and liquor as he was of sweets; he was allotted a keg of beer or a quart of whiskey a day.) Apparently people also considered him a sort of wishing well; when he died, hundreds of undigestible English coins were discovered in his stomach, along with a policeman's whistle and a set of keys. Jumbo was even saddled so visitors— including P. T. Barnum, on a visit to England—could ride him. He was the darling of the London Zoo, and especially of Queen Victoria, and he was treated accordingly. He had a personal keeper, Matthew Scott, to whom he was devoted, and a special mate, a much smaller elephant called Alice, whom he completely ignored.

But elephants in general, and Jumbo in particular, worried some zoo officials. Male elephants periodically undergo a condition called musth, when they are ready to mate. They can become aggressive, even violent. It was not unknown for a keeper to be badly injured, or even killed, by an angry elephant. Considering Jumbo's size, and the numbers of people who came daily to feed and pet and ride him, if he ever became unpredictably violent, it could mean disaster. In reality, Jumbo was usually gentle with people—but the zoo officials could not help being concerned.

It was inevitable that P. T. Barnum would want Jumbo, the biggest elephant alive, for his circus. In 1882, he offered the London Zoo ten thousand dollars for its most famous attraction. Worried about controlling an animal the size of Jumbo, the zoo accepted Barnum's offer.

England was outraged at the audacity of the brassy American showman. A movement spread to try to keep Jumbo in the London Zoo. The children who had fed the big elephant buns (and coins) and ridden on his back donated allowance pennies. Protesters composed songs, drew cartoons, and made speeches, pleading with zoo officials not to send England's beloved Jumbo to America. The hysteria of publicity rivaled the manias that had surrounded Tom Thumb and Jenny Lind. For a time, the huge beast became England's national pet, and national cause.

Jumbo did not seem to want to leave the London Zoo any more than his English admirers wanted to part with him. On the day Jumbo was scheduled to leave, his keeper led him out of the enclosure that had been his home for seventeen years. Beyond his familiar surroundings, the great Jumbo was as frightened and disoriented as a lost kitten. He lay down in the middle of the pathway, moaning and trumpeting piteously. Alice's sympathetic cries answered from her enclosure. Jumbo steadfastly refused to budge; he would not cooperate with the plan to parade him through the streets of London to the harbor, where he would board the ship for America. When Barnum heard about the commotion, he responded with his usual eye for publicity. Let Jumbo sit in the path as long as he wanted, Barnum ordered. It made headlines. Meanwhile, someone would think of a strategy to outwit the elephant.

Finally, Jumbo was led back into his pen. Each day after that, Matthew Scott walked Jumbo along a path, until it became a familiar, habitual stroll. At the same time, a cage on wheels was positioned on the walkway, and Jumbo was led through it until it was no longer strange or threatening. Then Matthew Scott took Jumbo for a final walk. When the elephant reached the middle of the cage, gates slid into place behind him, and the wheeled crate, pulled by ten horses, began to move. The first leg of Jumbo's journey to America had begun.

A trip by ship from London to New York took about two weeks. It must have seemed much longer for the people who had a six-ton elephant, occasionally seasick, as a traveling companion. Jumbo was kept placid throughout the passage with his daily ration of beer. (Barnum, still and always an ardent nondrinker, knew that his prize elephant didn't share his views on alcohol, but chose to ignore it. In one temperance speech, he even said that, if plain water was good enough for the largest beast on land, it was certainly good enough for people.)

Jumbo's arrival in New York was greeted with as much fanfare as his departure from England. The huge animal

Jumbo's arrival in New York City drew curious crowds. (Frank Leslie's, *April 22, 1882*)

quickly became a favorite attraction in Barnum's traveling circuses. Most of the other circus animals performed in acts; Jumbo, however, didn't do tricks. He didn't need to. His sheer size was what drew audiences: He continued growing to a height of twelve feet and a weight of seven tons. When the Brooklyn Bridge was opened, Jumbo was led across to test its strength.

The public loved elephants, and Barnum tried to provide them in all shapes, sizes, and even colors. He had been trying for some time to negotiate for a sacred white elephant from India, but they were so rare and so prized by their Hindu masters that his every attempt was sabotaged. Once a sacred elephant he'd paid for was mysteriously poisoned before it could be shipped out of the country, onto "heathen" American soil. Finally, however, Barnum's posters announced the arrival of Toung Taloung, a genuine sacred white elephant from Burma. What people saw was rare, but disappointing. Toung Taloung appeared to be an ordinary elephant, gray except for a pinkish white tinge around the trunk, with albino pink eyes. Barnum tried to educate the audience about the place of "white" elephants in Hindu culture, explaining how they were specially raised and treated with worship. But it wasn't enough for people expecting to see a milk white elephant. One of Barnum's circus competitors, Adam Forepaugh, tried to capitalize on the public's disappointment by displaying Light of Asia, an elephant who truly was a brilliant white in color—until the paint began to peel away.

Jumbo's life had been headline material. His death was, too. On the evening of September 15, 1885, Barnum's circus train was just preparing to leave St. Thomas, Ontario, after a performance. The elephants were being settled into their cars for the night; Jumbo was still walking about the yard. Suddenly, a locomotive came careening down the tracks. According to some reports, Jumbo charged the train headfirst. Other stories told of how the huge beast bravely shoved his handler and other human workers, along with a dwarf elephant he'd often marched with, out of the path of the hurtling engine. In any case, it was Jumbo, alone on the tracks, who sustained the impact of the locomotive, whose engineer was killed.

Jumbo was killed by a train in Canada in September of 1885. (Historical Collecti‍ Bridgeport Public Library)

An elephant, even a seven-ton elephant, is no match for a train, and Jumbo's huge skull was crushed. He died on the spot. Barnum, of course, was quickly notified at his home that his star attraction was dead. And he, making what he could out of the disaster, immediately called his taxidermists, to see if they could salvage Jumbo's valuable skeleton, or hide—or, preferably, both. For a dilemma had arisen.

In a menagerie as large as Barnum's, and with the art of zookeeping still a trial-and-error process, the showman had more than his share of dead animals. Many were also unusual and exotic, never seen before in America. For a long time, Barnum had an agreement with the Smithsonian Institution in Washington, D.C. The newly established museum would accept the stuffed, preserved specimens Barnum's skilled taxidermists brought it.

Then, in 1884, Barnum founded his pet project, the Natural History Museum of Tufts University in Medford, Massachusetts, where he was a trustee. More and more of his specimens were soon being donated to Tufts than to the Smithsonian. But he had never formally ended his agreement with the Washington museum.

Because of his great size, Jumbo was naturally of interest to scientists. They were sure to be curious about his remains. But at the time the elephant was killed, Barnum, Tufts, and the Smithsonian had not officially decided what was to be done with Jumbo in the event of his death. So Barnum sent his taxidermists to Canada with unusual instructions. Bringing the body back to Henry Ward's Natural Science Establishment in Rochester, New York, they were to try to preserve and stuff Jumbo's 1,538-pound hide. *And* they were to reassemble the two-ton skeleton, minus the damaged tusks, separately. Both the hide and the skeleton would be exhibited for a while in Barnum's circus: Since circus crowds had wanted to see Jumbo just because he was big, his remains would show his size as well as the live animal could. Afterward, the hide would go to the Tufts Museum. The Smithsonian ended up left out of the deal. Jumbo's skeleton would go instead to the American Museum of Natural History in New York City.

Barnum's plan worked. For a while, the circus displayed Jumbo's remains, hide and skeleton, side by side, with the elephant's "widow," Alice, still very much alive, standing by.

The twelve-foot-high skeleton of Jumbo is on exhibit periodically at the American Museum of Natural History. Jumbo, stuffed, was long the mascot of Tufts University, whose sports teams are called the Jumbos. But in 1975, a disaster all too familiar to P. T. Barnum struck the school. The Tufts Museum burned to the ground, destroying Jumbo's hide, Barnum's many other gifts, and a famed marble statue of the showman himself. Fire was a curse that haunted Barnum far past his own lifetime.

12

EGRESS

In 1880, a man named J. A. McGonagle sent P. T. Barnum a strange letter. There was a rumor spreading around Iowa, McGonagle said, that Barnum was dead. He was writing to find out whether the rumor was true. Barnum sent a quick reply: "My impression is that I am not dead."

Nevertheless, the world of the old showman had been changing dramatically since the 1870s. Charity Barnum had not been in good health for a long time. Her doctor advised fresh sea air. So the Barnums sold Lindencroft and built a new mansion, Waldemere, directly on Long Island Sound. The move did little good, however. On November 19, 1873, while Barnum was in Europe making a deal with a famous animal supplier, he received the sad news: Charity was dead. He went into seclusion for a few days, mourning privately, then went on with his business. The funeral service was conducted without him. The final interment in Mountain Grove Cemetery was delayed until he could return to Bridge-port—but he was in no hurry. The form of Unitarian religion

To be closer to the healthful sea air, Barnum built Waldemere overlooking Long Island Sound. (Historical Collection, Bridgeport Public Library)

Barnum professed promised a happy afterlife, and he was sure his patient, supportive Charity was in a good place.

Less than a year after his wife's death, Barnum shocked his family by remarrying. On his many trips to England, Barnum had become friendly with a man named John Fish. Fish gave all the credit for his success in business to Barnum's speech on "The Art of Money-Getting." He had two daughters, and it was the younger one, Nancy, who caught Barnum's eye, although she was forty years younger than her famous suitor. She was even younger than Barnum's daughters! Unlike Charity, Nancy appreciated fine theater and opera, and loved to travel. Barnum and Nancy Fish were married on September 16, 1874. Initially, Barnum's daughters were not at all happy with their father's decision, but they eventually accepted Nancy into the family.

Barnum wanted his young wife to have her own home, not something full of memories of Charity. He had Waldemere broken into three pieces, dismantled, and moved. Just a few yards away from the old foundations, he built Marina, his final, relatively simple Bridgeport home.

More sad news was in store for the old showman. In 1877, Barnum's youngest daughter, Pauline, came down with the measles. Diphtheria, a disease that blocks the windpipe, was raging throughout the country; already in a weakened condition, Pauline caught it. The diphtheria developed into

After Charity's death, Barnum married young Nancy Fish. (Historical Collection, Bridgeport Public Library)

pneumonia; the best doctors could do nothing. Pauline died on April 11, 1877. She was only thirty-one years old, and left behind a husband and three children.

Another of Barnum's daughters, Helen, caused something of a scandal. She had married a man named Samuel H. Hurd, who went on to work for his father-in-law. Helen was always the most impulsive of the Barnum girls, and she suddenly ran off to Chicago to be with William H. Buchtel, a doctor she'd met and fallen in love with. Divorce was far less common and accepted in the 1800s than it is today; despite the protests of her family, Helen divorced Hurd and married Buchtel, eventually settling in Colorado. Barnum remained on good terms with his daughter, occasionally traveling west to visit with her and his grandchildren. Meanwhile, former son-in-law Hurd continued to work for him.

In 1883, Tom Thumb, Barnum's earliest real success story and his lifelong friend, died in Middleboro, Massachusetts, and was buried in Bridgeport. Four years later, Jenny Lind—whom Barnum still sometimes contacted about doing another concert tour—was gone. One by one, his old associates were disappearing.

But new faces were taking their places. Barnum's grandchildren were growing up and having children of their own. Barnum called his great-grandchildren his "baby double grands," and delighted in amazing them with magic tricks from his Aaron Turner circus days, or taking them for pony cart rides around Sea-side Park.

Barnum seems to have believed that he would raise a second family with Nancy. He even revised his will to include any children he and Nancy might have. He especially hoped for a son; as he grew older, he wanted an heir for his business. And in the 1800s, it would have been very unusual—even

Barnum's final home was Marina. (Historical Collection, Bridgeport Public Library)

for a man as out of the ordinary as P. T. Barnum—to leave a complex business to a daughter rather than a son. But the years went by, and Nancy had no children. Barnum finally chose his grandson Clinton Hallett Seeley as the heir to his circus, on one condition. He wanted the family business to remain in the hands of someone with *Barnum* in his name. He insisted that Clinte legally change his name to C. Barnum Seeley, and the young man obliged. But his new name was the only thing that qualified him to take over his grandfather's circus. He had the reputation of being a playboy and was inept at business. Disappointed in Clinte's performance, Barnum was glad there were other good people to lead the circus, even if they were not named Barnum.

In 1883, Barnum discovered a new way to touch posterity. Thomas Edison had recently invented a wonderful device that could record and play back sounds, including the human voice. The machine would develop into today's phonograph and tape recorder. In the 1800s, however, Edison recorded his sounds on cylinders coated with wax. P. T. Barnum was one of the famous people of his day invited to record a brief message on the machine. Never able to resist a chance to advertise, he said, "I thus address the world through the medium of the latest wonderful invention, so that my voice, like my great show, will reach future generations, and be heard centuries after I have joined the great, and as I believe, happy majority."

In 1889, Barnum and Bailey's Greatest Show on Earth traveled to London. Perhaps sensing that it would be his last trip to one of his favorite cities, Barnum accompanied it. The British had never seen anything like the frenetic activity of a three-ring circus, and the show was a rousing crowd-pleaser. Barnum was in his glory, riding about the ring in his carriage at each show's conclusion, reveling in the applause and cheers. It was his last real moment of triumph.

In November of 1890, Barnum suffered a stroke. He was confined to his room in Marina, recuperating slowly, but he never really regained his strength. He put on a brave show of doing a bit of business from his bed, and his managers kept him informed of how the circus was doing, but he knew that his time was limited.

Since he'd published the first edition of his autobiography around the time of Jenny Lind's whirlwind tour, Barnum had revised it regularly, expanding on some stories and omitting others in each version. Soon he was putting out annual updates on his life, like yearbooks, which could be inserted into the original volume. The autobiography was sold door-to-door; copies had always been available at Barnum's two museums; and a person could hardly leave the circus without an

Barnum was the star of the show when he brought his circus to England in the final years of his life. (Barnum Museum, Bridgeport)

autobiography in hand, since there were always huge crates of the books available. Thousands of readers awaited the yearly installments. Barnum had a difficult request to make of his young wife. He asked Nancy, who was a competent writer, to compose and publish a final chapter to his autobiography after his death. She complied.

Barnum was the sort of man who would consider an obituary an advertisement—one that the person involved, unfortunately, would never see. So he was thrilled when the *New York Sun* contacted him with a bizarre idea. Would he like to see a sample of his obituary, in print—in an issue of the newspaper? Barnum, of course, loved the idea. On March 24, 1891, while P. T. Barnum was very much alive, the *New York Sun* ran his obituary for his approval.

Less than a month later, however, the announcements were real. Throughout April 7, 1891, Barnum was slipping in and out of a coma. He regained consciousness long enough to ask a typical Barnum question: How much money had the circus made that day at Madison Square Garden? Then, at 6:30 in the evening, after a few loving words to Nancy, he peacefully and painlessly died.

Not only had he preapproved his own obituary; Barnum had already selected a minister to preach at his funeral, along with the music he wanted played. He was buried at Mountain Grove Cemetery in Bridgeport, beside Charity and within sight of Tom Thumb's grave. The inscription on his gravestone was religious and oddly humble for the flamboyant showman: NOT MY WILL BUT THINE BE DONE.

A month after the burial, police were called to the cemetery. Vandals had unsuccessfully attempted to break into the grave, apparently trying to steal the body.

The day before what would have been Barnum's eighty-third birthday—July 4, 1893—there was an important unveiling at Bridgeport's Sea-side Park. A magnificent marble statue of Barnum had been carved for the museum he'd endowed at Tufts University. The artist's bronze copy, however, was given to Barnum's beloved city, and stood for many years at the entrance of the park he donated. Still attracting publicity one hundred years later, the statue was in the news in 1992, when vandals removed the bronze plaques from its pedestal. A few months later, the statue was moved temporarily from the park for repairs, and returned to its spot in 1994.

The Barnum touch is hard to avoid in the Bridgeport area today, with street after street named for members of his family. But he would be saddened and disappointed by the way the city he had such hopeful dreams for, the city he so wanted to develop and beautify, has decayed in recent years.

A statue of Barnum stands at the entrance to Sea-side Park, one of the showman's gifts to the city of Bridgeport. (Historical Collection, Bridgeport Public Library)

Hardly a trace remains of any of Barnum's four famed mansions. Iranistan's seventeen-acre farm where the elephant once plowed is now an urban area, the spectacular view down to Long Island Sound obscured by buildings. A high school stands on the land once graced by Lindencroft. Part of Waldemere is still lived in, in the neighboring town of Stratford, where it was moved when the home was divided. Finally, Marina, long since torn down, occupied a corner of property now owned by the University of Bridgeport.

At the time of his death, Barnum left money intended for a science museum, the Barnum Institute of Science and History, in downtown Bridgeport. The redbrick building with the distinctive turret now houses something closer to the showman's roots: the P. T. Barnum Museum. Besides galleries and displays where visitors can see Tom Thumb's miniature furniture and coaches, a scale model of a nineteenth-century circus, and a facsimile of the Fejee Mermaid, the museum hosts many special events connected to the world of entertainment in Barnum's day. The Bridgeport Public Library, established in part through Barnum's generosity, also houses an extensive collection of memorabilia.

And, while most American cities commemorate July 4 with parades, Bridgeport waits an extra day. Its annual celebration is held on July 5, the birthday of its most illustrious resident.

If Barnum were alive today, he'd certainly make creative use of modern media to update his infamous autobiography. Instead, others are doing the job for him. A television movie starring veteran actor Burt Lancaster presented the showman's life—fairly accurately—to millions. The Broadway musical *Barnum!* fictionalized many episodes, especially when it speculated on a romantic relationship between Barnum and Jenny Lind. But it captured the man's overwhelming charisma and enthusiasm, and the explosiveness of those qualities against the backdrop of the dull, placid society of early-nineteenth-century America.

Advertising has never been the same since P. T. Barnum perfected the art of "hype." People are interested in things like value and quality: Barnum never denied that. But first, they have to be stopped in their busy tracks by something that grabs their attention or catches their fancy or whets their curiosity—and won't let go. Barnum taught salespeople how to get noticed.

He was also an expert at giving people exactly what they never knew they wanted, from a silly laugh at a "cherry-colored cat" to an opportunity to hear the angelic voice of one of the finest operatic sopranos the world has ever known. Barnum had an uncanny sense for what would be popular, a talent for finding the best, and a gift for "packaging" and "selling" his discoveries. Today's business entrepreneurs, always looking forward to what people will want *tomorrow,* take their cue from P. T. Barnum.

In his long and colorful life, Barnum met a succession of presidents and dignitaries. Among them was General Ulysses S. Grant, commander of the Union forces during the Civil War and later president of the United States. When Grant, recently returned to the United States after a world tour, was introduced to the famous showman, Barnum remarked to him, " 'General, since your journey around the world, you are the best-known man on the globe.' "

" 'No, sir,' replied the General, 'your name is familiar to multitudes who never heard of me. Wherever I went, among the most distant nations, the fact that I was an American led to constant inquiries whether I knew Barnum.' "

The born Nutmegger had indeed become the Universal Yankee.

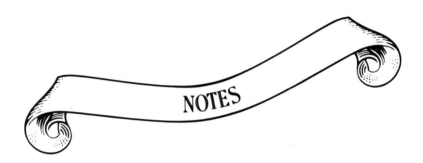

NOTES

Chapter 1

3   "Brass . . . I have none." P. T. Barnum, *Barnum's Own Story* (New York: Dover, 1961), 92.

7   "Universal Yankee Nation" *Barnum's Own Story,* dedication.

Chapter 2

9   "would go . . . under heaven." *Barnum's Own Story,* 3.

11   "I'd have . . . its seats." Felix Sutton, *Master of Ballyhoo: The Story of P. T. Barnum* (New York: G. P. Putnam's Sons, 1968), 13.

11   "had the reputation . . . in town." "I always . . . in my line." *Barnum's Own Story,* 6.

14   "all kinds . . . his neighbors." *Barnum's Own Story,* 40.

Chapter 3

22 "I did . . . money in him." *Barnum's Own Story*, 56.
25 "It was . . . notoriety." *Barnum's Own Story*, 71.

Chapter 4

35 "We have . . . establishment." *Barnum's Own Story*, 320.
37 "I am . . . crowing!" *Selected Letters of P. T. Barnum*, ed. A. H. Saxon (New York: Columbia University Press, 1983), 71 (2/14/1854).
39 "It is . . . *for it.*" *Selected Letters*, 26.

Chapter 5

44 "Prince of Humbugs," *Barnum's Own Story*, 102.
45 "Yes . . . shall again!" *Barnum's Own Story*, 107.
47 "had . . . plainly visible." *Barnum's Own Story*, 311.
48–49 "During . . . butchery." *Barnum's Own Story*, 404.

Chapter 6

56 "He is . . . Connecticut." *Barnum's Own Story*, 167.
58 "regardless of expense" P. T. Barnum, *Struggles and Triumphs or, Forty Years' Recollections of P. T. Barnum*, edited/abridged (New York: Penguin, 1981), 164.

Chapter 8

80 "I count . . . life." *Struggles and Triumphs*, 169.
82 "E-ternally." Irving Wallace, *The Fabulous Showman:*

The Life and Times of P. T. Barnum (New York: Alfred A. Knopf, 1959), 190.

82   "To . . . one." *Barnum's Own Story,* dedication.

Chapter 9

88   "All praise . . . things." *Letters,* 97 (3/9/1857).

Chapter 10

97   "a new . . . smashed up." *Letters,* 197 (3/20/1876).
99   "I *think* . . . patrons." *Letters,* 208 (8/3/1878).
101   "a real . . . every day." *Letters,* 197 (3/20/1876).
106   "You came . . . I'm Barnum." A. H. Saxon, *P. T. Barnum: The Legend and the Man* (New York: Columbia University Press, 1989), 235.

Chapter 12

115   "My impression . . . not dead." *Letters,* 213 (7/21/1880).
120   "I thus . . . majority." *Letters,* 335.
125   "General . . . Barnum." *Barnum's Own Story,* 440.

FOR MORE INFORMATION

Barnum, P. T. *Barnum's Own Story: The Autobiography of P. T. Barnum.* Combined and Condensed from the Various Editions Published During His Lifetime by Waldo R. Browne. New York: Dover Publications, 1961.

————. *Struggles and Triumphs or, Forty Years' Recollections of P. T. Barnum.* Edited/abridged. New York: Penguin, 1981.

Blumberg, Rhoda. *Jumbo.* New York: Macmillan, Bradbury Press, 1992.

Collins, Matthew. "The American Experience." PBS telecast, February 10, 1992: "Barnum's Big Top." Narrated by David MacCullough.

Cross, Helen Reeder. *The Real Tom Thumb.* New York: Macmillan, Four Winds Press, 1980.

Dodson, James. "The Myth Who Was the Man." *Yankee* 53, no. 9 (September 1989): 84–96.

Fleming, Alice. *P. T. Barnum: The World's Greatest Showman.* New York: Walker and Co., 1993.

Harris, Neil. *Humbug: The Art of P. T. Barnum*. Boston: Little, Brown and Co., 1973.

Hunt, Mabel Leigh. *Have You Seen Tom Thumb?* Philadelphia: J. B. Lippincott, 1942.

James, Theodore, Jr. "World Went Mad when Mighty Jumbo Came to America." *Smithsonian* 13, no. 5 (May 1982): 134–145.

Kaufman, Martin and Herbert. "Salamander the Fire Horse." *American History Illustrated* 15, no. 10 (October 1980): 36–38.

McCain, Diana Ross. "A Lilliputian Love Story." *Connecticut* 50, no. 2 (February 1987): 73–75.

Peterson, Robert W. "The Prince of Humbug: Showman P. T. Barnum Proved that Americans Love to Be Fooled." *Boys' Life* 79, no. 1 (January 1989): 22–25.

Preston, Douglas J. "Jumbo, King of Elephants: At the American Museum." *Natural History* 92, no. 3 (March 1983): 80–83.

Prideux, Tom. "The Imperishable P. T.; Subject of a Broadway Hit, Barnum Made Hokum an Art." *Life* 3, no. 7 (July 1980): 67–68.

"Psst! The Prince of Humbug Lives!" *U.S. News and World Report* 106, no. 24 (June 19, 1989): 16.

Robbins, Peggy. "When Jenny Lind Came to America." *American History Illustrated* 116, no. 6 (June 1981): 29–35.

Saxon, A. H. *P. T. Barnum: The Legend and the Man*. New York: Columbia University Press, 1989.

———, ed. *Selected Letters of P. T. Barnum*. New York: Columbia University Press, 1983.

Sutton, Felix. *Master of Ballyhoo: The Story of P. T. Barnum*. New York: G. P. Putnam's Sons, 1968.

Tompert, Ann. *The Greatest Showman on Earth: A Biography of P. T. Barnum*. Minneapolis: Dillon Press, 1987.

Wallace, Irving. *The Fabulous Showman: The Life and Times of P. T. Barnum*. New York: Alfred A. Knopf, 1959.

Ware, W. Porter, and Thaddeus C. Lockard, Jr. *P. T. Barnum Presents Jenny Lind: The American Tour of the Swedish Nightingale*. Baton Rouge: Louisiana State University Press, 1980.

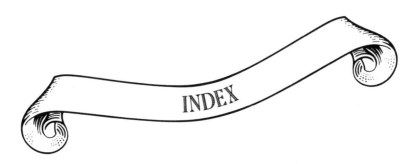

Page numbers in italics indicate illustrations.

Libel, Barnum's newspaper
and, 15
Lind, Johanna Maria ("Jenny"),
68–78, *70, 72,* 118
Lindencroft (Barnum home),
90, *91,* 115, 124
London Zoo, 107–109
Lotteries, 12–13
Lyman, Levi, 18–19, 21–22,
41–42

Marina (Barnum home), 117,
124
Mermaid. *See* Fejee Mermaid
Midgets, 51, 52–56, *54, 57,*
60–61, *62,* 66
Morality
of Barnum, 79–80
of entertainment, 28–29, 31,
68–69, 76, 79
of showpeople, 98–99
Museum Company, 4–6
Museums, 4–6, 29, 92–93,
113–114. *See also* American Museum
Music, 67, 68–69, 74–75

Native Americans, 25–26, 35–37
Natural History Museum of
Tufts University, 113–114,
123
New American Museum, 93–
94
New York Museum, 4–6
Newspapers, Barnum's, 14–15
Niagara Falls, 39, 45
Nutmeggers, 1–2, 7, 13

Nutt, George Washington
Morrison ("Commo-
dore"), 60–61, *62*

Obituary, of Barnum, 122
Olmsted, Mr., and American
Museum, 3–6
Opera, 67, 68–69, 74–75

P. T. Barnum Museum, 124
P. T. um's Museum, Me-
nagerie, and Circus, 95–
102
Panoramas, 34–35
Payment, for Jenny Lind, 69,
78
Performances, in circuses, 96–
98
Performers, circus, 99–100
Philanthropy
of Barnum, 85, 101
of Jenny Lind, 68, 77
Phonograph, Barnum's mes-
sage on, 119–120
Politics, Barnum in, 83–85, 91
Prince of Humbugs, 7, 44, 99
Product endorsements, 71

Railroads, 97, 111–113
Refreshments, circus, 99
Rings, in circuses, 96
Roberts, J. B. (juggler), 22–
24

Scott, Matthew, 108–109
Scudder's American Museum.
See American Museum